Shilappadikaram

படடெ

யுற்றே

கள்வெ

கொள்

Shilappadikaram

(The Ankle Bracelet)

By Prince Ilangô Adigal

Translated by Alain Daniélou

A New Directions Book

UNESCO COLLECTION OF REPRESENTATIVE WORKS

INDIAN SERIES

This book
has been accepted
in the Indian Series
of the Translations Collection
of the United Nations
Educational, Scientific and Cultural Organization
(UNESCO)

First published clothbound (ISBN: 0–8112–0246–1) and as New Directions Paperbook 162 (ISBN: 0–8112–0001–9) in 1965. Published in Canada by McClelland & Stewart, Ltd.

Manufactured in the United States of America.

New Directions Books are published for James Laughlin
by New Directions Publishing Corporation,
333 Sixth Avenue, New York 10014

SECOND PRINTING

The Ankle Bracelet

Introduction   VII

BOOK ONE: *Puhâr*   3

BOOK TWO: *Madurai*   69

BOOK THREE: *The Book of Vanji*   147

APPENDIX I: Preamble   207

APPENDIX II: Foreword of a Commentator   211

❧❦ INTRODUCTION ❧❦

India is a land of many races, many cultures, many languages, many religions. The origins of most of them are lost in the mists of ages so distant that we call it prehistory for mere lack of dated documents. Though many languages in India had very ancient literatures, they all came to be overshadowed by the development of Sanskrit, which became the language of Indian culture, not only because it was the language of the *Vedas* and all subsequent religious literature, but also because the various parts of India had constant need of a common tongue. Sanskrit, an "artificial language," as its name indicates, was derived from Vedic for this purpose; and it remains down to our day, though now in a more limited sense, the link connecting the various cultures of India.

Many ancient legends and myths and much historical information that we know today only through Sanskrit versions, came originally from non-Sanskritic sources. The great epics — the *Mahâbhârata* and the *Râmâyana* — and the myths and tales compiled in the vast encyclopedic works known as the *Purânas* (the Ancient Chronicles), probably belonged originally to other languages of India.

Among these non-Sanskritic languages, the only important ones that have maintained their independent existence and preserved their individuality until our day are the Dravidian languages, probably spoken at one time in most of India but later pushed down into the extreme south. Among these languages Tamil has maintained the greatest purity and has preserved some of its original literature.

We need not accept as fact the fabulous antiquity that South Indians often claim for the earliest poetical works in Tamil. But most scholars agree that ancient Tamil literature passed through three epochs, known as the Academies, or *Sangams*. Only the works of the Third *Sangam* have in part survived. According to Tamil tradition, this Third *Sangam*, extending over 1,850 years, ended in the third century A. D. The third century seems to the present writer to be accurate for the extant last works of the Third *Sangam*, but its opening date may have been set too early.

Five major poetical works in Tamil, usually called the Great-Poems *(Mahâ-kâvya)*, are attributed to the last part of the Third *Sangam* and subsequent centuries, i.e., between the third and seventh centuries A. D. These poems are really novels in verse. The texts of only three of them have survived, the most important being the *Shilappadi-kâram*, *The Lay of the Ankle Bracelet*. Composed toward the end of the Third *Sangam* it may have been slightly reshaped and enlarged during the following centuries.

The author of *The Ankle Bracelet* was Prince Ilangô Adigal, a brother of King Shenguttuvan, who ruled over the western coast of South India. This prince seems to have been a Jain. As we learn in the novel, all three of the great religions of India — Brahmanism (Hinduism), Jainism, and Buddhism — were at that time harmoniously coexisting in the south.

The *Ankle Bracelet* provides us with an astonishing amount of information about the civilization of the period—its arts, customs, religion, and philosophy—as well as a political map of South India and the names of a number of North Indian monarchs, which may, one day, permit us to date accurately the events it relates.

Already, however, certain internal and external evidence permits a reasonable estimate of its date of composition. The absence of any mention of the Pallavas in the south or of any paramount power in the north would indicate a date anterior to the Gupta-Pallava period. We know, furthermore, that Gajabâhu, king of Ceylon, who is mentioned in the *Shilappadikâram*, began his reign in 171 A.D. This would set the story near the end of the second century and its composition at the end of the second or the beginning of the third century. The date of 171 A.D. suggested by Ramachandra Dikshitar* for the composition of *The Ankle Bracelet* cannot be very far from reality. This does not exclude, naturally, the possibility of later additions. On the whole, however, the style and vocabulary of the work as we know it seem quite homogeneous and do not indicate multiple authorship.

There exist two commentaries on the text. One of these, the *Arumpadavurai*, by an unknown author, is ancient and incomplete; the other, by Adiyârkunallâr, was written in the fifteenth century.

This translation follows the Tamil text established by Swaminatha Aiyar. For difficult passages, I have generally kept to the interpretation suggested by the commentaries.

* Translator and editor of The Oxford University Press (1939) edition of *Shilappadikâram*.

For the identification of the names of plants, countries, and peoples, I have most often followed the *Tamil Lexicon* published by the University of Madras.

I was led to the study of *The Ankle Bracelet* in the course of my work on ancient Indian literature concerning musical theory. The interest of the novel seemed to me so great that I undertook its complete translation. The interpretation of the numerous technical terms on music in the text—many of which earlier editors had considered obscure—is based on my analysis of the theoretical possibilities of the ancient musical system, and on parallel theories found in Sanskrit works on music dating between the commencement of the Christian Era and the tenth century. Certain of these interpretations, however, remain hypotheses, and further research may produce a few variants.

I am very grateful to Mr. R. N. Desikan of Madras for his help in preparing the first draft of the translation, to Pandit N. R. Bhatt of the French Institute of Indology, Pondicherry, for his constant help and suggestions, and to Miss May Swenson, the late Sherry Mangan, Hayden Carruth, and James Laughlin of New Directions for their copy editing.

ALAIN DANIELOU

❧❧ BOOK ONE ❧❧

Puhâr

The Blessings

Mangalavâlttuppâdal

Blessed be the Moon!
Blessed be the Moon that wraps the Earth
in misty veils of cooling light,
and looms, a royal parasol
festooned with pollen-laden flowers,
protecting us.

Blessed be the Sun!
Blessed be the Sun that, endless pilgrim,
slowly circles round the axial mountain,
image of the royal emblem
of the beloved monarch of the land
where the Kâverî flows.

Blessed be the mighty clouds!
Blessed be the mighty clouds that on the Earth
shower down rain as generous
as he who rules the land
a raging sea surrounds.

Blessed be Puhâr, city of wonders!
Blessed be the city of wonders,
immortal testimony to the power
of a glorious line of kings
whose fame has spread to every land
the boundless sea surrounds.

Wise men, who study all that man can learn and know,
say that Puhâr, the wealthy river port, resplendent with

the fame of illustrious clans, once raised its head as strong and proud as Mount Podiyil, abode of the sage Agastya, and the peaks of the Himalaya. The splendor of the town rivaled that of heaven. Its pleasures were worthy of the underworld of the Nâgas, the divine serpents.

In this wealthy city lived Mânâikan, a famous shipowner, who was more generous than the clouds in the season of the rains. His daughter Kannaki was the most perfect branch ever grown from his tree. Though not yet twelve, she had the grace of a golden liana. The women of Puhâr all sang her praises. Admiring her virtues, they said: "She is beautiful as Lakshmî, goddess of Fortune, as she appears before the gods on her lotus throne. Yet she is more shy than Arundhati, wife of the sage Vasishtha, as she gleams, a tiny star, in the constellation of the Seven Sages."

In Puhâr there also lived a princely merchant named Mâshâttuvân, whose wealth was boundless. On him and on his parents the monarch had bestowed the highest honors of the realm. Possessor of vast treasure, he gave to the poor a good part of the wealth that his skill had gathered. This Mâshâttuvân had a son named Kôvalan, a youth of sixteen, whose growing fame had already traveled beyond the boundaries of the country.

Many a young maiden, with face gentle and pale as the new moon in autumn, would say to her trusted friend, in a warm voice made tremulous by heavy sighs: "Can there be any doubt that Kôvalan is really an incarnation of Murugan, god of Youth and Beauty?"

The noble parents of Kannaki and Kôvalan wished to see them united in the bonds of wedlock on an auspicious day. At this prospect their hearts were filled with joy and pride. They sent maidens of uncommon beauty, mounted on elephants, throughout the city to summon

4

with courteous words many a guest to a splendid bridal feast.

When, on the chosen day, the bride and groom advanced, white parasols shone high in the sky, as if for a royal parade, through streets echoing with the din of conch and drum. With youthful grace they entered together a pavilion of blue silk sown with pearls, its glittering pillars studded with precious gems and adorned with garlands of auspicious flowers. This was the day when the moon in the sky came nearest to Rohinî, the star of happiness.

Shyly, Kôvalan went round the sacred fire according to the Aryan rite, while the priest sang the fateful words. He approached his young bride, who, in her tender grace, stood humble as the faithful star Arundhati. Blessed were the eyes that could witness a sight so rare and delightful.

Gentle maidens with timid looks laid fragrant spices and odorous blossoms at their feet. Matrons with ample breasts and gleaming plaited hair carried scented powders, sandalwood paste, and incense. Ladies with smiling lips bore lamps and golden ware and tender buds of the hare-leaf *pâlikai*. Young women lithe as golden lianas, with flowers in their hair, scattered rose petals over the newlyweds, singing: "May your faultless love last eternally. May you lie forever on one couch, bound in the embrace of a love that shall never fade."

Then they led the tender Kannaki, the Arundhati of this earth, toward the nuptial bed. Leaving her, they withdrew, murmuring a prayer:

"May the tiger, emblem of our king,
carved on the Himalaya's golden peak,
forever stamp that king-of-mountains' brow.

And may the Chôla, our great king,
whose spear is sharp, unfailing in the fight,
uphold, before the nations of the world,
the golden discus, symbol of his power."

The Installation of a Home

Manaiyarampatuttakâdai

The riches of the Puhâr shipowners made the kings of
faraway lands envious. The most costly merchandise,
the rarest foreign produce, reached the city by sea and
caravans. Such was the abundance that, had all the world's
inhabitants been assembled within the city walls, the
stocks would have lasted for many years. The city spread
wide, vast as the capital of the northern Kuru—beyond
the Gândhâra country—where dwell sages famous for
their asceticism. Puhâr was unrivaled for the pleasures it
afforded and for the rare magnificence of its noble citizens, such as lotus-eyed Kannaki and her tender husband
Kôvalan, cultivated and endowed with inexhaustible
wealth.

   In one of the rooms of Mâshâttuvân's stately house
stood a large couch. Its legs, studded with precious stones,
were made with such art that they were thought to be
the work of Maya, the craftsman of the genii. During the
love-play of Kannaki and Kôvalan, the southern breeze,
drifting in through curtains sown with precious gems,
softly caressed their limbs. It wafted to them the hum of
the bees, the cool fragrance of lotuses, the scent of newly
open red lilies, the perfume of all that blossoms in field

and pond. It brought them the pleasing scent of *tâlai*, the intense odor of wide-open *kôdai*, while the bees, drunk with honey stolen from the warm heart of the champak, danced round the scented tresses and the smiling face of the happy girl.

Hand in hand, they went out on the breeze-swept terrace. There, in the moonlight, the god of Love was waiting with flowery arrows in his exquisite hands. The bees murmured songs to their ears while they lay on a bed strewn with fragrant pollen. On the naked shoulders of his bride, Kôvalan traced the form of a sugar cane, of which the bow of the god of Love is made, and a morning glory, the *valli*, which poets compare to a woman in love.

It seemed as if the Sun and Moon, for once conjoined, were blessing the sea-girt Earth with their interwoven light. Kôvalan was wearing a garland of jasmine buds, their hearts forced open by the bees; Kannaki, a wreath of blue lotus. In the ardor of their embraces the garlands became entangled. When he was satiated by love's pleasures, Kôvalan looked fondly at the radiant face of his new bride, and said tenderly:

"Beloved! To appear more handsome before the gods, Shiva adorned his brow with the fair crescent of the moon, but he lost this crown when the moon became your pale forehead. The limbless god of Love gave up his bow to make your dark eyebrows, for is it not the law of war that the victor takes his weapon from the vanquished?

"Leaving the gods at the mercy of the demons, Indra their king gave up his double-trident thunderbolt, that your waist might be wrought from its steel, for you are a treasure rarer than the life of the immortals. Against his nature, the beauteous young Murugan, six-faced god of War, gave up his fiery arrowheads so that your long eyes with their blood-red inner corners might frighten away the dark clouds of your hair. Shamed by your complex-

7

ion, the peacock ran into the woods to hide his jeweled robes. Radiant maiden, your sinuous walk so shamed the swan that now he stays hidden among the cool lotuses in the ponds.

"To hear your voice, soft as the ancient harp called *yâl* and sweeter than nectar, the green parrot keeps silent. Woman of noble gait, he perches, drunk with pleasure, on the flower of your hand.

"O girl with blossom-scented hair, the weight of jewels and the art of your maids add nothing to your loveliness. Save for those few flowers in your hair, what need have you of these heavy garlands? Why anoint with musk these tresses that the humble myrrh makes fragrant? Why these ropes of pearls when your breasts are already traced with arabesques of sandal paste? A foolish vanity has laden you with ornaments that bend your too frail waist and bring these tearlike pearls of perspiration to your tender brow. Set in pure gold, you are yourself a jewel without rival.

"You are the pure perfume, the sweet sugar cane, the translucent honey, on which I feast. Your grace is a ritual, your lips a spring of nectar. Noble maiden born of a noble line of merchants! You are a precious stone that has never known the darkness of a mountain mine. You are a nectar more fragrant than that distilled from sea foam, you are a harmony such as never arose from the strings of a harp. Your floating hair is darker than the night."

On the bed, strewn with broken garlands, the lovers spent sweet, pleasure-filled days in close embrace. Inspired by delight, he murmured in her ear choice blandishments coined with subtle art.

One day Kôvalan's noble mother thought of giving her dark-haired daughter a home of her own. She chose faithful servants and set aside ample wealth so that Kannaki might increase her renown by receiving relatives, wandering monks, and other visitors, in a manner suited to her rank.

As the years passed, Kannaki won great praise from all for the charm of her home, the grace of her hospitality.

> Image of Kâma and Rati,
> the god of Love and his consort,
> Kôvalan and Kannaki lay entwined
> like two black serpents on their couch,
> drank to its depths their cup of love,
> already having felt, perhaps,
> how transient is human joy.

✿❧ CANTO THREE ✿❧

Prelude to Tragedy

Arangérrukâdai

Agastya, a famous sage who dwells on the sacred Mount Podiyil, had once cursed the son of the god Indra and the nymph Urvashî for their unseemly behavior. But Urvashî was forgiven when she displayed her exquisite art on the stage. It was to this noble and adventurous pair that a beautiful girl named Mâdhavi was born. Her art as a

9

dancer was unequaled. Her shoulders were wide, and her flowing hair was always adorned with flowers. For seven years she studied dancing, singing, and etiquette, and became accomplished in all these arts. At twelve, she was asked to dance for the ruling monarch, and saw on his ankle the heavy circlet that only victorious kings may wear.

The teacher who had trained Mâdhavi was an expert in the two kinds of dance. He knew how to attune the rhythm of the body to the flow of the song. He taught the rules that keep the eleven positions of the breasts independent from the movement of the limbs. He knew the words of every song and could play every instrument. He was a faultless master of movement, gesture, composition, and rhythm. He knew which gestures should be made with one or with both hands, which movements are used for mime, and which belong to dance. Familiar with the most subtle secrets of this great art, he always kept the simple gestures separate from the complex, and never confused pure dance with character dancing. In footwork he carefully distinguished pure rhythm from rhythm suited to song.

Mâdhavi's music master was an expert performer on the harp and the flute. He could vocalize, and could draw from the drums well-rounded sounds, mellow and deep. He could adapt the music to the dance, and understood which style best suited each technique of expression. He had a profound knowledge of the subtle intricacies of the classical melodies, yet he could invent new variations. He taught the various styles of dance and of music, and brought out the most subtle shades of the composer's intention.

There was also in Mâdhavi's entourage a bard whose perfect Tamil was renowned in the Dravidian land that borders on the restless ocean. It could be seen from his works that he was a poet adept in the two forms of theatrical art, psychological drama and tragedy. A severe critic of all faults of style in the works of others, he knew how to avoid any flaw in his own.

The young drummer who accompanied Mâdhavi when she danced before the king was familiar with all the types of dance, musical notation, and singing. He knew prosody, modes, and rhythms, the blend of beats and counterbeats, and the defects that may arise from their contrast. He was well acquainted with popular tunes, and he could firmly establish the desired rhythm patterns on his drum, using an artful double stroke to mark important beats. He intertwined his rhythmic fantasies with the twang of the lute, the lament of the flute, and the soft accents of the songs. He controlled the voice of his drum so that the more delicate instruments could be heard, though, at the proper times, he would drown out all music under a deafening thunder of brilliant strokes.

The flute player of the group was also a scholar who knew all the rules of diction and the way that hard consonants are softened to please the ear. He knew four kinds of trills, possessed the science of modes, and adjusted his pitch to the deep sound of the *mulavu* timbal. He took care that the drums be tuned to the fifth note of flutes. He artfully followed the singers, improvising new variations within the bounds of modal forms, and showed his art of melody by setting off each note so that it might be clearly distinguished.

Then there was the harp master who played a fourteen-stringed instrument. To establish the mode *(pâlai)*, he first plucked the two central strings, which gave the tonic *(kural)* and octave *(târam)*. From these, he tuned the third *(kaikkilai)*; then the low strings from the octave and the high strings from the tonic. After tuning the sixth *(vilari)*, he played all the fourteen strings, showing all the notes of the mode from the low fourth *(ulai)* to the high third *(kaikkilai)*. The sequences that form the modes appeared in succession. Starting from the third, the scale of the mode *(pâlai)* known as *Padumalai* was obtained. From the second *(tuttam)*, he started the *Shevvali* mode, from the seventh *(târam)* the *Kôdi* mode, from the sixth *(vilari)* the *Vilari* mode, and from the fifth *(ili)* the *Mêrshem* mode. Thus the various groups of intervals were arranged. On the harp, the low sounds are to the left. It is the opposite with flutes. A good harp player is able to blend low and high tones with median ones in a manner pleasing to hear.

The site of the stage where Mâdhavi was to dance for the king was chosen according to the rules of divination. Soothsayers first studied the nature of the soil. To measure the stage, a *kôl* rod was made from a bamboo grown on a sacred hill. The space between each joint had to equal the span of the architect's hand. Its total length was twenty-four thumbs. The stage was eight rods long, seven deep, and one high. It had two doors. The wooden floor was four rods wide. In its center was placed the image of a genie before which the dancers gathered for dedication and prayer.

A very large oil lamp stood in front of the stage, so that the pillars would cast no shadow. The stage curtain, and the curtain over the door between the pillars on the right, were drawn aside by cords; so was the big drop curtain. There was a painted frontispiece from which were hung strings of pearls and other ornaments. Thus the stage on which Mâdhavi danced was both beautiful and novel.

The place of honor on the stage was reserved for the *talaikkôl*, a sacred rod made of bamboo. This phallic column, now used as the shaft of a magnificent parasol, was part of the booty that the monarch had taken from another proud and powerful king on the field of battle. It was gilded with pure gold from Jâmbûnada and in its joints were set nine different gems. The *talaikkôl* stood as the emblem of Jayanta the Victorious, son of the god Indra, and was the object of a cult in the palace of the royal Chôla, whose unstained parasol is borne high as the symbol of the security he ensures to the realm. Each time a royal dancer gave a performance, she sprinkled the sacred bamboo with holy water brought in a golden vase and wreathed it with garlands of flowers. It was then carried to the theatre on a huge elephant, whose broad brow was adorned with sheets of gold and draperies embroidered with glittering spangles.

To the sound of drums and horns, the king, accompanied by the five estates of his ministers, walked around the tall elephant. Then he handed the bamboo to the royal poet, seated alone in a chariot. All then went through the city in procession, and, entering the theatre, led the sacred *talaikkôl* to its place of honor.

The musicians sat in the aisle. The dancer, starting with her right foot, came in, stopping near the pillar on the right of the stage, in accordance with an age-old custom. Some older dancers stood near the pillars on the left. First two hymns were sung as a prayer that virtue might prosper and sin wither away. At the end of each verse the musicians loudly sounded all their instruments together. Then the harp was tuned to the flute, and the drum to the harp. The oboe gave its drone at the drums' pitch, and the cymbals were adjusted to match the clear sound of an earthen jar.

When all the instruments were tuned, the tempo was set as two strokes for one beat. Eleven beats were silently counted in accordance with a rule sacred to all actors. After an instrumental interlude *(antarakkottu)*, the auspicious prologue *(pâlaippan)* was sung without any change in tempo. The four parts of this short introductory song followed one another in the proper sequence. Begun on a ternary rhythm, it continued on a simpler one. On a graceful cadence the introductory dance ended.

Mâdhavi interpreted first a *Vaduku,* a northern dance from the Andhra country, then a variation on a fivefold rhythm. The two forms of the dance were merged into one of captivating loveliness. The dancer's movements were so graceful that she seemed a liana come to life. The perfection of her dance charmed the king, protector of the land. He gave her a wreath of green leaves and eight thousand *kalanju* gold pieces. Such was the gift, fixed by custom, that he presented, the first time they appeared before him, to those dancers worthy of carrying the sacred *talaikkôl.*

Deer-eyed Mâdhavi then ordered her hunchback maid to stand on the main street, where rich merchants pass, and offer them a wreath, saying: "He who buys this wreath of leaves for a thousand gold *kalanjus* shall become the master of my mistress, more supple and lithe than a liana." And on the wreath of leaves was painted the portrait of Mâdhavi, the lotus-eyed.

It was Kôvalan who bought the wreath, and, following the maid, entered Mâdhavi's apartment. When he took her in his arms, he felt a joy so keen that he forgot everything and could not leave her. He forgot his faithful young wife and the unstained name of his house.

Frail ankles bejeweled with circlets,
Mâdhavi, that beauty of Puhâr,
displayed upon the stage her dance,
her precise diction, subtle sense of time,
her knowledge of all rhythmic patterns,
of the five sorts of temple songs,
of the four systems of music,
of the eleven kinds of dance.
Her fame spread to the ends of the world.

⚘ CANTO FOUR ⚘

The Sunset

Antimâlaissirappucceykâdai

The twilight had come on. Clad in her oceans, the Earth
was lamenting in plaintive tones, like a widow who has
abandoned herself to her grief:
"No longer can I see the unchallenged discus of my
Lord, emblem of his power, spreading its light over land
and sea. Where is the Moon whose cool radiance dispels
the darkness of the sky?" Earth's four faces paled, tears
filled the flowers of her eyes, beads of sweat covered her
prostrate frame. As a criminal chieftain leading his rebels
raids the country while the king is away, carrying disaster
into the homes of loyal subjects, so the evening triumphantly stormed the ancient city of Puhâr. It brought
with it grief to faithful wives whose husbands were away,
and joy to those waiting to meet their secret lovers. This
was the hour when the shepherd plays the song of the

forest on his flute, when the bees tumble down, drunk on the blood of wild jasmine.

The soft southern breeze gently brushed the brutal six-legged bees away from the tender buds they were trying to force open so as to release their secret fragrance to the air. Girls with gleaming anklets were preparing the lamps.

It is said that all Pândya kings, from youth on, have the power to drive away all enemies. Now, like them, their ancestor the Moon appeared and put the twilight to rout. The silvery king of the stars, without debasing his pride, spread over all men his milky rays.

The couch of Mâdhavi was strewn with wild blossoms from the forest, fragrant jasmine, and odorous petals. In the love chamber she seemed unaware that her girdle was undone and her thin garment slipping from her lovely hips. Lustful, she came out onto the terrace bathed in moonlight. All night only loving quarrels would interrupt the passionate embraces of Kôvalan.

Mâdhavi was not the only one blessed with love's sweet joys. The breeze gently caressed many a lotus-eyed woman lying voluptuously against the strong chest of her lord. Before falling asleep, the women burned incense, blending the white *ayir* from the western hills with the black *agar* from the east. They anointed their bodies with sandalwood paste from the southern mountains, crushed on northern sandstone. They wore garlands of leaves, twined with lotus stalks and blossoms, and blue water lilies interwoven with strings of pearls. In the ardor of love, the pollen fell on beds strewn with fragrant petals.

But the heart of Kannaki was oppressed by sadness. No anklets adorned her shapely feet. No girdle held in the folds of the light plain garment wrapping her tender hips. No costly vermilion had been used to color her breasts. She wore no ornament other than her beauty. No jewel brightened her ears, no pearl of perspiration adorned her moon-pale face, no eye-black lengthened the line of her fish-curved eyes, no red mark glowed on her forehead. The tender smiles that once had been Kôvalan's delight had long abandoned her lips. No sweet oil burnished the dark curls of her hair.

Women, separated from their beloved lords, sighed heavily, like squeezed-out goatskins. They withdrew from their summer apartments into darkened winter rooms. Their grief was the more bitter because they dared not adorn their breasts with sandal paste and strings of pearls. No longer might they lie on couches strewn with flowers gathered in the gardens and the humid meadows, or on beds made of the soft white down the swan casts off at mating. Unhappy women, who in tender quarrels with passionate lovers had rolled their eyes from nose to ears, became addicted to the melancholy of loneliness. Pearl-like tears fell from their reddened eyes.

The shimmering lake, spread out before their eyes, seemed a graceful maiden: the silent wake of the swans was her walk, the honey-laden flower buds her fragrance, the opening lotus her rosy lips, the waves of black sand her long hair, the red water lilies her eyes; the bees were serenaders waking her at dawn, the rooster a messenger from her love the day. At times, the birds in the sky cried out like conchs blown or drums beaten, to announce that dawn was coming to lift the darkness from the sleeping city, spread wide as the murmuring ocean.

When dark grew deep, the god of Love,
his pennant bearing a symbolic fish,
came wandering vigilantly through the town,
holding his bow of sugar cane
and arrows made of flowers.

Indra's Festival

Indiravilavûréduttakâdai

The Sun appeared, peering over the eastern hills. He tore off the mantle of night, spread his warm and friendly rays over the pale Earth, which seemed a lonely virgin, uncomely and forlorn. The ocean waves were the folds of her robe, the hills her breasts, the rivers her strings of pearls, the clouds her disheveled hair.

The sunshine lighted up the open terraces, the harbor docks, the towers with their loopholes like the eyes of deer. In various quarters of the city the homes of wealthy Greeks were seen. Near the harbor seamen from far-off lands appeared at home. In the streets hawkers were selling unguents, bath powders, cooling oils, flowers, perfume, incense. Weavers brought their fine silks and all kinds of fabrics made of wool or cotton. There were special streets for merchants of coral, sandalwood, myrrh, jewelry, faultless pearls, pure gold, and precious gems.

In another quarter lived grain merchants, their stocks piled up in mounds. Washermen, bakers, vintners, fishermen, and dealers in salt crowded the shops, where they bought betel nuts, perfume, sheep, oil, meat, and bronzes. One could see coppersmiths, carpenters, goldsmiths, tailors, shoemakers, and clever craftsmen making toys out of cork or rags; and musicians, expert in each branch of the art, who demonstrated their mastery in the seven-tone scale on the flute and the harp. Workmen displayed their skills in hundreds of small crafts. Each trade had its own street in the workers' quarter of the city.

At the center of the city were the wide royal street, the street of temple cars, the bazaar, and the main street, where rich merchants had their mansions with high towers. There was a street for priests, one for doctors, one for astrologers, one for peasants. In a wide passage lived the craftsmen who pierce gems and pearls for the jewelers. Nearby were those who make trinkets out of polished nacre and sea shells. In another quarter lived the coachmen, bards, dancers, astronomers, clowns, prostitutes, actresses, florists, betel-sellers, servants, oboe players, drummers, jugglers, and acrobats.

In wide fields near the town were encamped horsemen and their swift mounts, war elephants, chariot drivers, soldiers fearful to look upon. Near these were palaces of knights and princes. Between the quarters of the workers and the nobles lay an open square, large as a battlefield where two great armies might have met. There, under rows of trees, the sheds of a market were set up. The haggling of buyers and sellers could be heard there all day long.

On the first day of Spring, when the full moon is in Virgo, offerings of rice, cakes of sesame and brown sugar, meat, paddy, flowers, and incense were brought by nubile girls, splendidly dressed, to the altar of the genie who, at the bidding of Indra, king of heaven, had settled in the town to drive away all perils that might threaten Muchukunda, its ever-victorious monarch. Hands on their generous hips, these virgins gyrated madly as if possessed by obscene devils, and then in a circle performed the dance of lust, the *Rasa-lîlâ*, which the god Krishna had performed with the cowgirls. As they went away from the altar, the dancers cried: "May the king and his vast empire never know famine, disease, or dissension. May we be blessed with wealth — and, when the season comes, with rains."

Brave warriors, billeted in the workers' quarters, and army commanders, living in noble homes, crowded near the altar, shouting in harsh voices: "May danger flee before our valiant king. O genie, be ever with us warriors, come to honor thee with hecatombs!"

The slingers and lancers, their shields fouled with blood and human flesh, beat their shoulders with shouts of joy. It seemed that their ferocious red eyes might burn to ashes any on whom they should alight. Offering their fierce heads to the sacrificing priest, they cried, "The king will return victorious!" and their dark hairy heads fell upon the altar. The roar of the raw-leather drums seemed to be their voices howling back from afar: "Accept, O great genie, our lives, offered to thee in sacrifice!"

Once King Tirumâvalavan wandered along all the frontiers of his realm, vainly seeking a monarch deserving the honor of battle. In the far north, he thought, he might meet adversaries more worthy of his sword. So on an auspicious day he ordered that his lance, his parasol, and his war drum be brought. He prayed to his genie, asking for the favor of an opponent mighty enough for his shoulders. Then he marched northward and ever northward until only the Himalaya, the abode of the gods, was able to stop him. There he carved on the face of the king of mountains his own emblem, the lion, and returned in glory.

The king of Vacciranâdu, whose empire extends eastward to the boisterous sea, offered him as tribute a dais studded with pearls. The king of Magadha, deft in swordplay and hereditary enemy of his clan, gave him an audience hall. The king of Avanti, as token of his submission, presented him with a sumptuous archway. These gifts, heavy with gold and gems, made with a skill unknown to the best of craftsmen, were the work of Maya, the architect of the genii, who had once given them, for some service rendered, to the ancestors of these kings. When their gifts were all gathered together, they formed a harmonious ensemble, admired by all men of taste.

The town of Puhâr possessed a spacious forum for storing bales of merchandise, with markings showing the quantity, weight, and name of owner. Since there were no doors or guards, robbers might have been tempted. But there was an invisible watchman, a genie, who blinded any would-be thief so that he was left staggering about with his burden on his head, unable to find his way out. Hence, at the mere thought of stealing, everyone was struck by fear.

There was a miraculous pond, where the lame, the mute, the deaf, or the leprous, by bathing in its waters or walking round it, could recover beauty, strength, and health. In an open square stood a tall polished monolith. Men driven mad by an excess of drugs, paralyzed by poison, bitten by sharp-toothed snakes, or possessed by ghosts, found instant relief by walking round it and worshiping it. There was a crossing of four roads where lived a fierce genie. His voice could be heard ten leagues away when he shouted that he would bind, beat, and devour imposters dressed as monks to dissimulate their misdeeds, crafty women addicted to secret vice, dishonest ministers, lewd seducers of others' wives, and all bearers of false witness and gossip. There was also a square where stood a rare statue, the lips of which never parted, but which shed tears when the monarch transgressed the law or failed to render justice. In these five notable places daily sacrifices were offered by wise people who understood their mystery.

The drum of augury, taken from the temple of Vaccirakôttam, was carried on a colorfully caparisoned elephant to the temple of the white elephant. This rite announced the commencement of the feast of Indra. A great banner picturing a white tusker was raised high in the air before the temple of the wishing tree.

Wooden stands had been constructed on the balconies of the great mansions. They were studded with emeralds and brilliants, and had pillars of coral. At the entrance to each mansion were placed hangings embroidered with sea dragons, and elephant tusks bearing auspicious marks. Strings of pearls swung from large and artfully wrought rings. In the streets, gold vases filled with water and amphorae of glazed pottery had been set out as for a marriage feast. Metal lamps shaped like girls, golden flags, feather fans, scented paste, and fragrant flower festoons were everywhere to be seen.

Then there assembled the royal councilors of the five estates, the eight bodies of courtiers, the princes, the sons of noble merchants, swift horsemen, elephant drivers, and the charioteers who carry to far-off lands the dominion of the glorious monarch. From the estuary of the Kâverî, one thousand and eight kings brought on their heads jars filled with the sacred water, scented with fresh pollen. With this water the image of the god of gods was bathed, for the joy of earth and the glory of heaven.

The people made merry on Indra's chosen day. Great rituals were performed in the temples of the Unborn Shiva, of Murugan the beauteous god of Youth, of nacre-white Valiyon, brother of Krishna, of the dark Vishnu, called Nediyon, and of Indra himself, with his strings of pearls and his victorious parasol. A festive crowd invaded the precincts of the temple, where Vedic rituals once revealed by the god Brahmâ were faultlessly performed. The four orders of the gods, the eighteen hosts of paradise, and other celestial spirits were honored and worshiped. Temples of the Jains and their charitable institutions could be seen in the city. In public squares, priests were recounting stories from the scriptures of the ancient *Purânas*.

The king's chariot, its banners flying, passed triumphantly, reminding all of how the king had subjugated his rivals. Through the city oboes and tambourines could be heard. The voices of the bards blended with the soft accents of the harps. Night and day the rhythm of drums filled every corner of the city with merriment.

Joyful to be near her lover, beautiful Mâdhavi, her ears weighted with precious rings, lost nothing of her charm. A soft breeze from the hills wafted the odor of wild and garden jasmine, of *mayilai*, of blue water lilies, and of the aphrodisiac purple lotus to Mâdhavi, herself the rarest of flowers.

Charmed by the sight of the lovers' rapture, the breeze wandered through gardens of delight faintly scented by tender buds too shy to open yet; it roamed through the market noisy with frolic, where it gathered the perfumes of incense and sandal paste; and, entwining itself with the laughter of lovers, it scattered their secrets as it passed. Gently warmed by the young summer, it kept company with wandering bees, whose murmur resembles the *ili*, the fifth note of the harp. And like the breeze, Kôvalan too wandered through the busy streets with singers, oboe players, and companions expert in seeking adventure.

One of the young men thus celebrated his beloved lady:

"The Moon, in fear of Râhu, monster who
devours her on the days of her eclipse,
fled from the sky in search of shelter.
Framed in the dark clouds of your hair,
she reappeared then as your pallid face.
She chased away the hairs from your fair cheeks,
painted two soot-black fish-shaped eyes,
and in the middle placed a *kumil* flower,
that since then passes for your pretty nose."

Another lover sang to his love:

"You are a lightning-flash, born in the sky,
that Eros, a fish upon his pennant, hurled
when he descended on this earth in search
of his annihilated body, drinking all the nectar
that the pale Moon distills us drop by drop."

Another sang:

"Once a lotus, with its honey-brimming heart,
seeking its mate, that goddess Fortune,
disguised itself as two shoots of black hemp,
growing at each side of a *kumil* flower.

It blossoms also in the jasmine's form
and in the red flower of the cotton tree,
showing that Fortune has set up her camp
in this our wealthy city, favoring a king
whose power covers all the universe."

And still another sang:

"Are you, though costumed as a girl,
Yama, Death's Lord, destroyer of all life,
who, out of fear of our most virtuous king,
discarded his male semblance, thus to hide
under your bashfulness? And does he smile
and speak, through your lent voice, those words
more tender than a harp's sweet notes?"

With their frivolous talk, the broad-shouldered gal-
lants won easy victories over their lady-loves, though all
were virgins, chaste as the unshakable Arundhati. Like a
battalion in which every man was an Eros, they captured
the fleeing girls and held them tight in their arms. Their
broad chests were streaked with the red sandal with which
the girls painted their breasts. Pleasure and restless nights
reddened the women's lotus eyes that once were white
as water lilies. Virtuous citizens asked: "If offerings to
the genie do not cure the malady that reddens the eyes
of our girls, where is a remedy to be found?"
    The great day had arrived when the king of the gods
is honored. The dark left eye of Kannaki, and the red
eyes of Mâdhavi suddenly filled with tears and their lids
began to flutter, Kannaki's with sorrow and Mâdhavi's
with joy, just as the blue water lily trembles and pales
when honey overflows in its heart.

On the Beach

Kadalâdukâdai

Once the god Vidyâdhara, he who is called the Angel of
Wisdom, in the fragrant garden of Chedi, the celestial
city on Kailâsa, the Mountain of Pleasure, was celebrating the feast of Eros with his beloved, she of the long
fish-shaped eyes.

He suddenly realized that the festival of Indra, king
of gods, would begin on this day in the far-away city of
Puhâr. He said to his love:

"Let us go visit that famous site where a great genie
comes to feast on sacrifices offered in thanksgiving, for,
on orders from Indra, he once diverted arrows shot by
the Titans against Muchukunda, the victorious monarch
and hero among men, whom fear had disabled while,
tigerlike, he kept watch at the gate of Amarâvati, the
capital of Paradise.

"There we can see the five halls of assembly, famed
for their splendor. Gifts of Indra, and symbols of his grat-
itude, they were built for the present king's ancestor, who
kept watch at his gate.

"Once the fair nymph Urvashî danced before Indra
the thousand-eyed. But a melody played by the sage Nârada on his harp so displeased the prophet Agastya that
he cursed both musician and dancer:

"'May the dancer be reborn
and the harp be silent.'

"And that is how Mâdhavi was born, with a pubis like a cobra's hood. We shall go to see her dancing.

"Wasp-waisted girl with coral lips! Come to the festival of the king of heaven."

They set out, and on the way he showed his beloved the countless peaks of the Himalaya, the ever-abundant Ganges, the city of Ujjain, the forest of Vindhya, the hill of Venkata, and the plain of the Kâverî, rich in fields. Soon they reached the city of Puhâr, nestling among flower gardens. After they had worshiped the image of Indra with the prescribed ritual, he showed her the city. They took part in all the ceremonies and games of the festival, held in this oldest and richest of cities.

The god said:

"Let us hear the hymns to Vishnu, and the prayers sung to the genii of the four castes. And, after these, the people will sing a ballad to the moon that wanders through the sky for the benefit of all men.

"Near the fair Umâ, who beats the time, you will see Shiva dancing in a graveyard the dance of Destruction and the swift dance of Time—the same that he performed with faultless rhythm, at the request of all the gods, when an arrow of fire, guided by his will, destroyed the three flying cities of the Titans.

"You will see the white dance of Shiva, in woman's attire, before the four-faced Brahmâ standing on his chariot, the elephant dance that dark Krishna performed after upsetting the perfidious designs of King Kamsâ, and the wrestler's dance he performed after killing Bâna, the black demon. You will see also the dance of triumph of the god of Youth, Murugan, using the ocean as a stage, danced after he killed Shûra, who had taken refuge in the ocean's depths; the parasol dance, in which, to slight

27

them, he lowered his white parasol before the routed Titans coming to surrender their arms; the dance of the amphora that Vishnu, with his long stride, performed when wandering in the streets of the great city of Bâna; the epicene's dance that the god of Love performed after giving up his male form to become a hermaphrodite; the war dance that the goddess Mâyaval performed when the depravity of the Titans became unbearable; the dance of the statue that Lakshmî, the goddess of Fortune, performed when the Titans surrendered their weapons and gave up the fight; and the bracelet dance that the consort of Indra performs in the fields near the northern gate.

"You will see, beloved, these various styles of dancing, accompanied by songs, that dancers in costume mime with gestures, keeping their bodies erect or bending them, according to the rules of their art.

"Look! There is Mâdhavi, who claims descent from the illustrious Mâdhavi I mentioned while we were still in our garden scented with most fragrant pollens."

Thus spoke the wise Vidyâdhara, charmed at the prospect of the coming spectacle.

Kôvalan was in quarrelsome mood, sorry to see the end of Indra's festival, with its carnival, its dances, and its constant tinkle of anklets, which even the inhabitants of heaven came incognito to attend.

To please him, Mâdhavi bathed her fragrant black hair, soft as flower petals, in oil mixed with ten kinds of astringents, five spices, and a blend of thirty-two pungent herbs. She dried it in the smoke of incense and anointed each tress with heavy musk paste. She then adorned her tiny feet, their soles dyed red, with well-chosen rings on each of her slender toes. She loaded her ankles with jewelry made of small bells, rings, chains, and hollow anklets. She elaborately ornamented her shapely thighs, fastened round her hips a girdle of thirty rows of pearls set on blue silk and embroidered with figures and flowers. Armlets studded with pearls, and bangles made of carved precious stones, embraced her arms. Priceless bracelets, on which rare stones were set among sparkling diamonds, shone over the fine down on her wrists. Above and below the bracelets she wore slender circlets, too: some of fine gold, others of the nine auspicious gems, still others of coral beads, and one of pearls. Her rosy fingers, delicate as *kântal* flowers, disappeared under ornaments shaped like fish-jaws, and under rings of dark rubies and flawless diamonds. Her frail throat was adorned with a chain of gold, exquisitely wrought, and with a garland. She wore also an ornament of precious stones, held by a loop, which covered the nape of her neck and her shoulders, as well as earrings of emeralds and diamonds. Shell-like jewels called *shîdêvi, toyyakam,* and *pullakam* were woven into her black tresses. Within her elaborate love-chamber, she offered Kôvalan pleasures ever renewed and the joys of tender quarrels.

Very late one night under the full moon she noticed that the people of the ancient city were walking toward the beach in search of amusement. Mâdhavi, scented with *talai,* thought of following them. This was the hour when the swan's call is heard among the lotuses of the ponds, when the cock takes his brilliant trumpet to summon the dawn, when the star of love shines high in the sky, and when darkness is prepared to die.

Kôvalan adorned his broad chest with jewels and flower garlands. Looking like a generous cloud, he mounted his mule, while doe-eyed Mâdhavi climbed into her ox-drawn carriage. They crossed through the bazaars lined with tall buildings in which millions of bales of precious merchandise were stored. Beautiful lamps shone everywhere, some adorned with flower garlands. Young women with glittering jewels were scattering flower petals, fresh blades of grass, and tender shoots of rice on their well-polished floors, to bring good luck to their homes. The goddess of Fortune had indeed settled in this street, where people liked to wander all day long.

The lovers crossed the main street, with its warehouses of merchandise from overseas. Then they came to the low-lying quarters near the sea, where flags, raised high toward the sky, seemed to be saying: "On these stretches of white sand can be found the goods that foreign merchants, leaving their own countries to stay among us, have brought here in great ships." One could see the booths of dealers in colors, shoes, flowers, perfumes, and sweets of all kinds. Farther on, the lamps of the skillful goldsmiths were shining, and those of the porridge-sellers, seated in rows. Peddlers of trinkets had heavy black lamps raised on stands. Farther on were the lamps of the fishmongers.

Near the shore lighthouses had been built to show ships the way to the harbor. Far away one could see the tiny lights of the fishing boats laying their nets in the deep sea. All night lamps were burning, the lamps of foreigners who talk strange tongues, and the lamps of the guards who watch over precious cargoes near the docks. Bordered by rows of aloes, the seashore was more enchanting even than the fields with their lotus ponds and streams. The lamps gave such abundant light that one could have found a single mustard seed had it fallen on the clear sand, spread evenly like fine flour.

Surrounded by her friends and maids, Mâdhavi passed near the harbor, where the ships, laden with the produce of the mountains and the sea, lay sleeping. At one end of the beach the princes were standing with their courtiers, and the noble merchants were busy with their agents. In a canvas enclosure dancing and singing girls were hidden.

The colorful garments, the din of voices, recalled the tumult of the first festival, when Karikâla, the great king whose renown reached heaven, celebrated the freshet of the Kâverî, surrounded by the four castes of his people crowded on the narrow strip of land where the great river weds the sea.

Long-eyed, flower-soft Mâdhavi took from the hands of Vasanta-mâlâ, her maid, a harp of rare melodiousness. Then on the fine sand, carefully spread under a tall mast-wood tree, in a small enclosure planted with pandanus, whose fragrance veiled the strong smell of the sea, on a white bed, surrounded by a screen and overhung by a canopy adorned with suggestive pictures, Mâdhavi gave herself up to pleasure in the strong arms of Kôvalan.

✨ CANTO SEVEN ✨

Songs of the Seashore

Kânalvari

Mâdhavi paid homage to the harp, then lifted off the embroidered covering that protected the body, neck, and strings of the completely perfect instrument. Covered with wreaths, the harp resembled a young bride, whose dark eyes are made darker by eye-shadow.

Mâdhavi then carefully followed the eight rules of perfect music: the tuning of the instrument *(pannal)*, the caress of the strings to indicate the mode *(parivattanai)*, the exact pitch of each note *(ârâidal)*, the duration of rests *(taivaral)*, the grave adagio *(shelavu)*, the easy blend of the words of the song *(vilaiyâttu)*, the sentiment *(kaiyûl)*, and the elegant design of the vocalization *(kurumpôkku)*.

Her fingers, wandering on the strings with plectra carved in emeralds, evoked a buzzing swarm of bees when she practiced the eight ways of touching instruments: the isolated pluck *(vârdal)*, the caress *(vadittal)*, the hard stroke to bring out the resonance *(undal)*, the passage from one string to the next *(uraldal)*, the presentation of a theme *(uruttal)*, the pull on the string to reach the note from above *(teruttal)*, the chords *(allal)*, and arpeggios *(pattadai)*.

Then Mâdhavi handed the harp to Kôvalan, saying: "It is not for me to give you orders, so may I inquire at which rhythm I shall accompany your songs?" To her joy, he began to sing an ancient ode to the Kâverî, followed by lusty sailors' songs.

ODE TO THE KAVERI

Long live the Kâverî! When the royal Chôla,
white wreaths embellishing his moonlike parasol,
departed to impose upon some far-off foreign land
the scepter of his justice, falls in love,
upon his homeward way, with the lovely Ganges,
you must not frown, for people say, O fish-eyed beauty,

that to retain your smile although he courts the Ganges
is just the greatest asset of all faithful wives.

Long live the Kâverî!

And when our monarch, with his unstained parasol
adorned with garlands of fresh flowers, starts
his march to bring to far-off lands
protection of a scepter never known to bow,
and marries on his way the virgin of the south,
Kanyâ Kumârî, Cape of the Virgin, at India's southern tip,
you must not yield to sadness, O Kâverî,
for I have heard it said, O fish-eyed river,
that to keep smiling when he courts
the virgin of the cape is far
the best of policies for a faithful consort.

Long live the Kâverî!

O Kâverî! You roam about the fields,
and listen to the ploughman's vulgar songs,
and to the lock-gates' wail,
the call of waterfalls,
the clamor of a festive crowd
that's come to celebrate your freshet.
The patience of our king, whose soldiers' tongues are
sharp, with your unchaste behavior, shows his heart is
good.

Long live the Kâverî!

THE SERVANT GIRL TO HER MISTRESS'S LOVER

Good day, my lord!
How can we, small people, understand
why some unscrupulous gentlemen
so often lead our mistresses,

33

whose eyes are like dark flowers,
to the altar of the sea god, there
to lavish pledges never kept?
We're from Puhâr, where water lilies smile,
and open when you show them pearls,
or even bracelets of cheap nacre, which
they surely take to be the Moon
or some star pouring milky rays.

How can we know, my lord, who are
the men who follow us along the strand?
Their hands are heavy with their presents,
but they prove to be odd foreigners who
expect us to pay dearly for their gifts.
We're from Puhâr where demented bees mistake
the blue eyes of its girls for lotus blossoms
gazing along the moonlight's path.

We're from Puhâr where conchs from the sea,
bruised by the shameless waves,
are thrown upon the beach and crash
upon sand-castles that our girls have built.
The flowers fall out of their undone hair.
Angry, they tear the lilies from their wreaths
to beat the shells. And passers-by,
at sight of all these flowers, take them for
alluring glances from unnumbered eyes.

THE LOVER'S FRIEND

To hide the furrow in the labored sand,
in which a conch-shell is concealed,
the *punnai* tree lets fall upon the shore
its pollen-heavy flowers.
Fish-shaped eyes set in a moon-pale face

may cause a languor only to be cured
by tender touch of sandal-painted breasts.

SONG OF THE FAIRY

A youthful maiden, wreathed with flowers,
taken from the tender jasmine vines,
is struggling with a black bee-swarm.
She means to drive away the birds
attracted by the strong smell of her fish
spread out to dry upon the sun-warmed beach.
Really she is a fairy who has come
out of the fragrant garden of the genii.
If I had known she might be near at hand
I never should have dared to come.

OTHER SONG OF THE FAIRY

Beside the fisherfolk's low huts there lies
a terrace where the nets are left to dry;
and Death, concealed within a young girl's form,
her eyes as sharp as deadly arrowheads,
sits on the shore, there where the shining sand
is beaten by the lustful waves. She holds
a wreath of lovely flowers in her hand,
and sells her fish. Had I been told
she might be near, I had not dared to come.

THE LOVER'S SONG

Here is the perfect picture of them all:
the Moon's become a face, with black

fish painted on it for its eyes,
a bow for brows, and clouds for hair,
in which the power of Eros hides.
Tell me, is it true that when the Moon
fled the fierce dragon that devours it in eclipse,
it found a refuge in a fisherman's hut?

These eyes are spears. See their points stained with blood,
piking some conch the sea has cast away.
For us they are the direst peril of them all.
For cruel Death, disguised as a lithe, frail girl,
has come to live here in a fishing hamlet
on the shore of the restless sea.

Look there!—a woman trying to disperse
birds crowding near her drying fish. And all
who see her feel a curious malady. She is
a lewd, fell goddess feigning a naïve village girl;
her hair is parted, modest, in five braids,
and she sits on sharp-pointed hare-leaves,
spread on the shore of the fearful sea.

THE LOVER TO HIS CONFIDANT

The fragrance of a garden's flowering shrubs,
the soft cool smell of vast extents of sand,
the chosen words uttered by tender lips,
rich youthful breasts, a moonlike face,
a brow's fine arch, a waist thin as a thunderbolt's
challenge the painter and induce my grief.

A sandy shore, raped by the waves,
wastes of pale sand,
flowers that spread their cloying fragrance far,

the pleasant shade of trees,
the scent of long hair all undone,
a moonlike face with carp-shaped eyes,
have filled my heart with melancholia.

A beach with gathered shells in heaps,
the breeze's fragrance in a garden,
soft petals falling from too opened flowers,
secret retreats that she alone has found,
young teeth like freshest *kumil* buds,
a face to which the Moon alone can be compared,
and tender breasts — all these induce my grief.

BOY TO GIRL

Your elders do their fishing in the sea,
and live by killing blameless creatures there.
You do your fishing in my heart,
and live by causing me to die.
Oh pray, be careful not to break
your waist, too frail to bear the weight
of young breasts growing opulent!

Your father kills the buoyant fish
caught in the ambush of his net.
But you delight to kill all living things
caught by your lovely eyes' most deadly snare.
Oh pray, be careful not to break
your waist, thinner than thunderbolts,
for it may yield beneath its load
of heavy breasts and strings of pearls!

Your brothers in their swift canoe
go hunting creatures that have done no harm.

But you kill with the arched bow of your brows;
your fame increases with the grief you cause.
Oh pray, protect the slimness of your waist,
that's growing strong beneath the burden of your breasts!

A COMPANION TO THE LOVER

A girl, eyes reddened from her sleeplessness,
holds in her hands a coral pestle. She
crushes white pearls in her little mortar.
The greedy eyes of a girl crushing pearls
cannot be compared with innocent lilies.
These red eyes are cruel.

I saw a girl with reddened eyes,
advancing with a swan's slow gait
under the shade of *punnai* trees
along the putrid and wave-beaten shore.
The red eyes of a girl, pacing the shore
with a swan's gait, are fearful and bring death.

A red-eyed girl, heavily garlanded
with purple honey-laden flowers,
tries to disperse the birds who congregate
around the nets that dry in the warm sun.
The red eyes of the girl who tries
to chase the birds — they are not harmless darts,
but deadly arrows shot at us.

ANOTHER SONG

Witless swan! Keep away!
Do not come near!
Your gait cannot compare with hers.

Innocent swan! Do not approach!
Do not come so near to her!
You never can compete.
Stolid swan! Remain far from her!
Her game is men, and, for the hunt,
she haunts the confines of the earth
encircled by a tremulous sea.
Oh, keep away!

Long-eyed Mâdhavi had patiently listened to all
these sailor songs. But she felt they showed a change in
Kôvalan's feelings. Angry but pretending to be pleased,
she took the harp. To change their mood, she sang an
ancient ode to the river, of a beauty so startling that the
Earth goddess was bewitched. All those who could hear
marveled at her skill and were charmed by the sweetness
of her accents, the blend of her voice with the vibrant
sounds of the harp.

ODE TO THE KÂVERÎ

Hail, Kâverî!
Robed with flowers, swarmed by singing bees, you roam,
sinuous and fanciful,
casting dark glances from your swift
and carplike eyes.
Your gait and charming looks are the pride
of your lord, whose virtuous scepter's never gone astray.
Hail, Kâverî!

Hail, Kâverî!
When you meander through the countryside,
swinging your hips to rhythms of a flower wreath,

the peacock dances in the fields,
the cuckoo shrieks with joy.
I heard it said that your enticing gait,
when you go wandering to your garlands' swing,
was learned at point of a strong husband's spear.
Hail, Kâverî!

Hail, Kâverî!
Just as a mother feeds her child,
throughout the ages, you have fed the fertile land
of a king whose fortune shall remain
until the furthest end of time.
The blessings that you shower on our dear land
are fruits of the wheel of justice
held by our monarch, scion of the sun.
Hail, Kâverî!

SONG OF PUHAR

Sir! Like the god of Love you come
and try each day to give us pearls.
Your pearls have not the brightness
of our dear lady's spotless teeth
set between coral lips in her moon-white face.
We're from Puhâr where an ambitious sea
barters its brilliant pearls against our wreaths.

Gold bracelets on the shapely arms
of sturdy daughters of our fisherfolk
show they are married, but in secret.
Naïve, we fail to understand.
We're from Puhâr, where water lilies
hiding the bustling bees within their hearts,
open their petals when they see a swan,
perched on a blossoming *punnai* tree,
thinking it is the moon among the stars.

40

In this our country, where the good wine
makes him who drinks of it so drunk
he cannot hide his drunkenness,
how can we know why there's no remedy
for that queer enlarging malady you cause our girls.
We're from Puhâr, where a male sea rapes
the sandy castles that we girls construct,
and eyes, as sharp as spears, on full-moon faces,
shed bitterest regret's too tardy tears.
We take up sand by handfuls, throwing it
against the impudent waves, trying to fill the sea.

SONG OF THE HEROINE

Although he well can tell between
a male crab and a female one—
and he saw me in a garden thronged
with clusters of sly flowers—
a prince of the coastal province,
with all discernment lost, no more
takes any interest in girls with five plaits.
He went away, taking what he sought,
on his swift chariot that a fine horse drew,
and gave me never another thought.
O gracefully flowering hare-leaf vine!
O swan! Let him go far. But we
cannot forget him who's forgotten us.
And like my eyes, at twilight shedding tears,
O heavy *neydal* flower, honey-laden,
you know not pain nor sleep's sweet peace.

In dreams you do not see a dear
hard-hearted boy speeding along the shore.
When he set out, a bird in flight,

on his swift horse-drawn chariot,
the limpid water of the sea
soon wiped away the traces of his wheels.
O innocent waves of the sea!
You cannot understand my plight.
Who can assist me if you help
those who throw mud at my good name
with words more than unkind?
—waves that so soon efface the ruts
cut out by lovers' strong, broad chariots.
Cool shade! Tall swan courting his mate!
O wave-wet strand! Can you not tell my love
how wrong his conduct may appear?
O blessed waves! you who erase the traces
of the chariot of my love,
you wipe away his memory,
yet claim to be my confidantes.
Unfriendly waves! I shall forever leave you.

THE MAIDSERVANT TO THE GIRL'S LOVER

The sea, adorned with coral and
with strings of faultless pearls,
has sent its waters far into the fields.
O ruler of the sea! In the white *punnai*-flowering garden
the arrow shot by dragon-mounted Eros
seems to have changed our mistress's lithe form.
What shall we do then when her mother sees it?

O prince of the seashore!—where the strong waves,
showing their teeth of pearls
between their coral lips,
enter the courtyard where the fishers' nets
lie drying in the sun. What will occur
when soon the mother of this blameless girl,

seeing her pale as the yellow *pîra* flower
that blossoms when the weather's cold,
asks the diviner and finds out the guilty one?

O prince of the seashore!—where the strong waves
sweep off the smell of fish from the beach,
and, entering the flower gardens' coolth,
ebb backward, freighted with sweet-smelling blooms.
My youthful mistress is observed to pine
under an ailment of a cause unknown.
What shall I do then when her mother learns
the true name of her curious malady?

A GIRL TO HER MAID

Night spreads its darkness on the grieving earth.
The maker of the day has gone.
My eyes are filled with tears. My sorrow cannot die.
You, my maid with flowers in your dark hair, say:
Is this fiery sunset, that drives me mad
and swells the golden bracelets on my wrists,
seen in the country where the dear deserter is?

The sun is vanishing and darkness spreads.
From unguent-heavy lids the hot tears fall.
My lovely maid with a young moon's face!
Tell me, is the wandering twilight that has come,
vomiting a pale moon and eating up the sun,
seen in the country where the dear boy's gone?

Birds' songs are ended now,
the ruler of the day has gone.
Unending tears are tedious for pretty eyes.
Maid whose tresses are decked with flower buds!
Tell me, does this maddening twilight come
from the country where the absconder lives?

Walking through the marsh, a lad
came through the garden's thick
pandanus hedge, and disturbed our love-play.
He went away, thus having spoiled our joys,
but left my heart gnawed by a newer love.

Through the marsh, beside the garden, near the sea,
someone drew near us secretly, and said, "Be kind."
Now everywhere our doe-eyes seek to find
the boy who asked us to be gentle to him.

And he who yesterday was looking at
a swan who made love to his mate,
he who all yesterday was waiting there, today
can now be driven from our hearts no more,
as a dark mole cannot be torn away
from our flesh.

TO THE CRANE

Go away, crane! Leave the garden!
Do not come near! Stay far away!
You have not told my love,
the prince of the seashore,
the torment that I suffer.
Go away, crane! Leave the garden!

After these songs in Kôvalan's manner, the lovely
girl's rosy fingers drew from the harp eight secondary
modes. She played *kaikkilai*, short variations on the
theme of unhappy love, taking as the tonic the first, lowest, string *(kural)* of the harp. Then, in faultless style, she
improvised a melody *(pân)*.

A GIRL SINGS TO THE TWILIGHT

Evening! In the pleasantly descending scale
sung by seafaring men,
you brought together thirds and fourths,
irreconcilable enemies.
Evening! If you create harmony
between a third and neighboring fourth,
I am prepared to give away my life.
May you be pleased and endure forever.

Evening! You deprive of their illusion
those who seek consolation
in remembrance of the promises
of lovers taking leave.
When you surround them, cruel Evening, you are like
a conqueror laying siege
to the fortress of an enemy king.

Evening!—that renders me insane. You sneak in
when the ruler of the day has gone away,
bringing sadness to a world that only asked
to close its eyes and to forget.
You trouble my thoughts and someone drives me mad.
The earth is sad, the evening demented. Be at peace!

THE MAID INVOKES THE SEA-GOD
SO AS TO BE OVERHEARD BY THE LOVER

Lord of the sea! I bow to your lotus feet.
Once on a fiery and unkind evening
that drove us all quite mad,
our lover left, forgetting oaths
he made before you in a flowery garden,
and his sweet words misled our anguish.
May you forgive his lack of faith.

45

While he listened, Kôvalan thought: "I sang only fairy tales, but this perfidious girl has woven lies into a song made for some other love." Inspired by fate, for whom the harp appeared a suitable pretext, he gradually withdrew his hands from her body, radiant as moonlight. He said: "The day has ended; the time has come to depart."

But she remained motionless upon the couch.

When Kôvalan had gone with all his retinue, Mâdhavi rose. She stopped the babble of her maids, and left the flowered enclosure. Seated in her carriage, she went back to her home, alone and sad. She sang:

> The Chôla monarch Shembiyan
> rode on an elephant brilliantly adorned;
> compelled the monarchs of the earth
> to bow themselves before his feet
> in terror of his sword of fire;
> and spread his flower-garland-laden
> parasol's protecting shade up to
> the earth's encircling mountains.

𝒻𝓀 CANTO EIGHT 𝒻𝓀

The Approach of Spring

Vênirkâdai

The celebrated god of Love, with Spring, his gracious friend, ruled the fertile Tamil land, that spread from the northern Venkata hills, where Vishnu the savior of the world resides, to the southern virgin sea. The country had four capitals: Urandai the luxurious, Madurai of the high ramparts, Vanji the strong, and Puhâr the guardian of the sea.

The approach of Spring was announced by its messenger, the south wind, blowing from green Mount Podiyil, that peak sanctified by the stay of Agastya, the sage all men respect. As if trumpeting the order—"Soldiers of the dragon prince, dress ranks!"—the cuckoo, bugler of the great army of Eros, sounded its shrill notes through the dense forest, which a curtain of creepers made impenetrable.

After her break with Kôvalan in the flowery pleasure grove by the sea, blossom-eyed Mâdhavi came back alone to her rich home, and climbed to her summer refuge, a tower near the sky. For her own pleasure, the elegant girl decked her heavy saffron-powdered breasts with pearls from the southern sea and sandal from the hills. Holding her faultless harp, she sang a tender melody that filled her heart with grief. Then, to forget, she sat in the lotus posture.

Her right hand on the harp's body took the flag position (pataka); her left hand lay resting on the instrument's neck (mâdagam). She was expert in sounding various notes strongly (ârppu), softly (kûdam), or tenderly (adirvu), avoiding all dissonances. She played the fourteen notes of the classical scale, beginning with the fourth (ulai) in the lowest octave, and ending with the third (kaikkilai). She carefully searched for the exact pitch of each note, tuning the second (inai) on the fifth (kilai), the sixth (vilari) on the third (pakai) and the fourth (natpu). She sang, using as drone the harp's fifth string (ili).

47

Then she sounded the fifth and seventh *(târam)*, beginning and ending first on the fourth, later on the tonic *(kural)*. She practiced the four groups of modes *(marudam)*, the *ahanilai*, the *puranilai*, the sixteen-stringed *maruhiyal*, and the *peruhiyal* with its thirty-two notes. Careful of the three shades of pitch, high, median, and low, that may color the notes, she played some graceful melodies *(tirappan)*. Soon this flowering liana felt weary and started elegant variations *(venirpâni)*.

She then made a garland of champak, mixed with *mâdhavi, tamala,* jasmine, and fragrant roots, in which perfect lilies alternated with the red petals of hooked pandanus flowers. Taking a long bamboo stylus, she dipped it in a writing paste made of lacquer mixed with glue, and inscribed a message inspired in her by Eros, who, armed with his flowery shafts, was imposing his rule upon the world:

THE LETTER

Spring, the world's worst tyrant,
is an irresponsible lad
who hurls one on another
most ill-assorted lovelorn hearts.

Though not free of defects, the Moon
arises, kindling ardent wants
that evening soon makes unendurable.
Eros may well, in sport,
assail with deadly flower-darts
a few hearts that are lonely,
be they lovers that have parted, or
those waiting for a certain one's return,

or former lovers who have gone away,
the once dear cherished face forgot.
Please try to understand my pain.

Thus pale Mâdhavi, perfect in the sixty-four arts,
wrote on the wreath, showing the naked depth of her
passion. While she was carefully writing, she hummed,
like a small child, a mode *(pân)* and its prelude *(tiram)*.
When the evening had brought her peace, she sent
for Vasanta-mâlâ, her handmaid, and bade her go to
Kôvalan, to repeat before him all the words inscribed on
the wreath of flowers, and to bring him back to her arms.
Vasanta-mâlâ, who had long eyes like arrowheads, carried
the garland to Kôvalan's home near the grain merchants'
residences. She herself placed it in his hands.

Kôvalan refused the garland and murmured:

"A dancing girl in love once performed the prelude
(kankûduvari), with a red mark on her brow and flowers
in her hair. Her thin eyebrows were dark; her eyes, resembling two water lilies, sent alluring glances. Her nose
was like a *kumil* bud, her lips a *kovvai* flower.

"Then this girl with the long dark eyes showed us
an inviting variation, the *kânvari*, coming forward but
shyly withdrawing again, her moonlike face oppressed
by the weight of her hair, heavier than the rain clouds.
Her eyes were like quivering carps, and her enticing
smile showed the pearls of her teeth set in the coral of
her lips.

"She next revealed a character-dance *(ulvari)*. Her
piercing eyes were sharp as spears: she could well see
that after our quarrel I was desperate and forlorn.

"Feeling weary, at the hour of low tide, she appeared
disguised as her own servant girl, comforting me with

49

words sweeter than a parrot's. Her walk was as graceful as the swan's, her grace subtler than the peacock's.

"Intoxicated by desire, she danced the brief, lewd dance of lust *(puravari)*. Her frail body could not bear ornaments: she danced on the steps of my home to the rhythm of her swaying belt, the music of her ankle bells. She knew I desired her but would not embrace me. She performed the dance of indignation *(kilarvari)*. Her innocent forehead was framed by curls of the hair which, with its load of flowers and pearls, whipped her shoulders. The weight of her breasts forced her frail waist to bend. She appeared unconcerned that her tresses were undone. When a messenger placed at her feet a letter telling her my love, she feigned to misunderstand it.

"Then she danced the theme of anguish *(têrccivari)*, crying out to the four winds the pain caused her by our parting and the unbearable desire that draws her toward me. She committed the impropriety of revealing her anguish to members of my family. Next, wearing a wreath that drew swarms of bees to her, she performed the dance of despair *(kâtcivari)*. She told her misery to all the passers-by. She pretended to faint *(eduttukkôlvari)*, and, more than once, did lose consciousness. Those into whose arms she fell recalled her to her senses and tried to comfort her.

"But for this girl, adorned with jewels, whom I once dearly loved, such dances are a daily performance. She is only a dancing girl."

When Kôvalan refused to take the wreath that the beautiful and jewel-laden Mâdhavi had sent him, and the message written on its *tâlai* and pandanus flowers, Vasanta-mâlâ was overwhelmed with grief. She ran to her mistress to tell her all that had happened. But Mâdhavi of the long flower-eyes answered her:

"Lovely girl, if we do not see him today, he will
come tomorrow at dawn."
Yet with heavy heart she lay sleepless all night on her
couch strewn with fresh flowers.

CODA

Vasanta-mâlâ speaks

When Spring comes, the red lotus blooms,
the mango's tender leaves begin to tremble,
the noble *ashoka* bursts into flower.
Who can describe the pain that lingers in
my mistress's tender eyes, shaped like sharp spears?

The cuckoo trumpeted his command:
"All lovers who have quarreled
shall rush into each other's arms.
For so does Eros order."
You enjoyed her tender words
in that enclosure by the sea,
but shut your ears to the appeal she wrote
on those frail petals this day when her heart
was ravished by the frenzy of the Spring.

CANTO NINE

The Dream

Kanâttiramuraittakâdai

Evening approached, the day faded away; women, their
waists lithe as lianas, scattered grains of paddy and open
jasmine buds on the floors of their homes. They lighted

51

lamps studded with glowing gems. And they changed into the clothes they wear at night.

Once, long ago, Mâlati gave a cup of milk to the young son of the second wife of her lord husband. The boy choked, had spasms in his throat, and died. She was terrified, for she knew that her Brahmin husband and his new wife would unquestionably accuse her. She took the dead child in her arms and carried it to the temple where the *kalpaka*, the "tree of ages," is worshiped. From there she ran in succession to the temples of the white elephant, the pale god Bâlarâma, the Sun, Shiva the god of the City, Murugan the spear-bearing god of Youth, Indra who wields the thunderbolt, and the god who dwells beyond the city walls. She also visited the Jain temple and the temple of the Moon. She beseeched all the gods:

"O mighty ones! Give me your help in my terrible trouble!"

At last Mâlati reached the sanctuary where the famous god Shâttan had made his residence. Shâttan was skilled in the art of magic; she resolved to ask his advice. At that moment a young woman appeared—a girl of such startling beauty that she made all others look plain. She said to Mâlati:

"Innocent girl! The gods do not grant their favors without a sacrifice. This is no lie but truth. Give me the child."

With the words, she snatched the dead body from the startled woman and ran off into the darkness toward the funeral pyres. There the demon Idâkini, ravener of corpses, seized the child and devoured it. Mâlati shrieked like a peacock at the roar of thunder. The divine Shâttan came and tried to console her:

"Mother, be calm! Give up all fear! Look straight before you and you shall see the child come back to life."

To fulfill his promise, the god took the form of a boy asleep beneath the cuckoo-haunted trees. Mâlati, mad with joy, grasped this supposititious child. She clasped it to her heart and brought it back to its mother.

This divine Brahmin boy grew up and became learned in all the sacred scriptures. At his parents' death he observed with piety the rites to ancestors. He was so wise that people made him a judge in their quarrels. He married a woman of uncommon beauty named Devandi. Before approaching her, he prayed:

"May the flowers of your eyes be able to withstand the fire of mine!"

One day he revealed to her the fact he was immortal, and then, requesting her to visit his temple, he disappeared. Before he left, he had taught her certain mysterious magic words. After that, Devandi went each day to worship him in his sanctuary. To those who asked news of her husband she would say:

"He has gone on a pilgrimage. If you meet him, please bring him back to me."

She had once heard about the unhappy life of virtuous Kannaki, the loyal wife abandoned by Kôvalan; it saddened her. Bringing to the god an offering of *arugu* grass and rice, she beseeched him to intervene. She went to Kannaki, blessing her:

"May your husband return!"

Kannaki replied:

"He may come back, but my trials will not end. I had a fearful dream. The two of us were walking hand in hand toward a vast city. Some people told a lie, so that Kôvalan was accused of a crime. When I heard it, I felt as if I had been bitten by a scorpion. I ran to the king, and threatened him and his city with disaster. I should say no more. It may be only a bad dream. O woman with narrow bracelets, when you hear about the harm done to me and its happy results in the end for my husband and me, you may laugh."

Devandi said:

"Woman with gold anklets! Your husband did not reject you. All this is the result of a vow that remained unfulfilled in a past existence. To counteract the curse that vow has brought upon you, you should visit the sacred site where the Kaveri flows into the sea. Near a few *neydals* in blossom there are two ponds, dedicated to the sun and moon. Women who bathe in these ponds and then worship the god of Love in his temple shall spend all their lives close to their husbands and later enjoy the pleasures of Paradise. So let us go bathe there today."

Kannaki at once answered the well-meaning woman:

"This plan is not proper: [a married woman should worship no other deity than her husband]."

A few moments later, a young servant approached and said:

"Our dear Kôvalan has come to our door. It seems that from now on he will look after us."

Kôvalan entered. He was struck by pain when he saw the pallor of the graceful Kannaki. He said:

"Living near a woman bred on falsehood and for whom truth and untruth are alike, I have lost all the wealth my ancestors gathered. I feel great shame at the dire poverty that I bring into this house today."

Welcoming him with a clear smile that lit up her face, Kannaki said:

"Do not be anxious: you still possess the gold circlets that weigh on my ankles. Accept this modest gift."
Kôvalan answered:
"Honest girl! I accept these precious ankle bracelets as a new capital from which we shall regain all the jewels and all the riches I have squandered in my folly. Let us get ready, woman with the flower-adorned hair! Come! We shall go to Madurai, a city known for its towering walls." Inspired by fate, he decided to start at once, before the day should come to disperse the night's dark veil.

CODA

The nightmare of a faithful wife
emptied of their purport the words
of Mâdhavi, whose oval eyes were dark.
Before the Sun should dissipate
the darkness of the night, they left,
impelled by fate that had devised
for ages past their final destiny.

✿❦ CANTO TEN ✿❦

Country Sights

Nâdukânkâdai

Darkness covered all things during this last quarter of a tenebrous night. The sun's eye was not yet open in the heavens. The moon had left the brilliant circle of the stars. Led by fate, Kôvalan, accompanied by his young wife, started his long journey.

55

They left the house through the high gate, closed by two huge, heavily locked doors on which a carved goat, yak, and soft-feathered goose wandered together in friendship. They walked around the great temple sacred to Vishnu, the sapphire-hued god who sleeps, in omniscient unconsciousness, on a great serpent coiled to form his bed. They passed near the five-pillared halls built by Indra, where the saints of heaven, who come by aerial paths, teach the Law of Dharma that the Buddha revealed when he preached under the tree of wisdom, whose five branches point toward the sky as the symbols of knowledge.

They walked around the highly polished black stone installed by the Jain citizens as a pulpit for the wandering *châranar* monks who come to the temple on festive occasions. These monks would arrive on the days when the river began to rise or when the huge temple car was pulled out in procession. They sat on the high stone platform, under the golden shade of their sacred *ashoka* trees in bloom. There was the meeting-point of the five aims of life, sought for by the five kinds of yogis. Near the monks were assembled other virtuous ascetics who, according to their vow, could never eat flesh or tell a lie. Purified of their sins, masters of their senses, they had found the true path leading toward liberation.

The travelers passed the postern, winding through the high walls like a stream in a mountain gorge. They reached the parapet beyond a moat that enclosed the royal gardens. The great trees were in bloom, and they seemed a tribute sent to the king by the god of Love through his two messengers named Spring and Mountain Breeze.

They followed a broad avenue leading to the steps that descend into the stream where people come to bathe.

The avenue was lined with huge trees spreading their cool shade far and wide. Walking westward for about ten miles, they reached the dense forest that covers the northern bank of the river, often swept by the Kâverî's floods. They saw a grove of trees in bloom, where a saintly nun named Kavundi lived. The frail girl with the fragrant hair had already lost her breath and felt weary. Her feet were bleeding. Showing her teeth in a faint smile, she asked in a faltering voice if they were yet near Madurai, the great city. Kôvalan laughed gently. Concealing his emotion, he replied:

"Woman with the five fragrant plaits, it is not too far off — only three hundred miles from our ancient city!"

They went to pay homage to the venerable and saintly Kavundi. Both humbly prostrated themselves at her feet. Seeing them approach, the saint welcomed them with gentle words:

"You both appear handsome, wellborn, and well-mannered. It seems that you observe with care the rules of life prescribed by the holy books of the Jains. Why then are you in distress, why did you leave your home to travel in this wilderness?"

Kôvalan said:

"We have no tale to tell. We are going to the ancient city of Madurai, saintly woman, to seek our fortune."

The saint answered:

"The tender feet of this girl cannot stand the roughness and the sharp stones of this path. Such a beautiful young woman should not travel in the forest. Yet, even if I so asked you, you would not give up your venture. I too have always wished to visit Madurai, the stainless town of the southern Tamil land, renowned for its beauty. There I could pay homage to Arivan and listen to the Law being taught by the holy monks who, through their severe penance, destroy all traces of evil in their hearts. I shall come with you. Let us set out."

Kôvalan bowed before the venerable saint. Raising the palms of his hands, he told her:

"Saintly woman! If you do us this great favor, my fears for this girl, whose feet are adorned with ornate anklets, will be greatly lessened."

"But I must warn you, Kôvalan," Kavundi answered him, "that you will meet many hardships on the way. Listen! If we take the road that wanders below the flowering trees, so as to protect this delicate girl from the burning rays of the sun, we may not be able to avoid the deep trenches that are dug by the eaters of some roots that people here call *valli*, which grow deep under the earth. Often these holes are hidden under heaps of faded flowers. But, intent on watching for these piles of petals, you may hit your head against the heavy breadfruits that are hanging from the trees. Or, going through the rich land where ginger and saffron are grown, you may step upon the sharp hard breadfruit seeds that lie half hidden in the dust.

"Tender husband of the lady with the carp-shaped eyes, should you prefer to go through the fields, she will be frightened by carp-chasing otters quarreling in the ponds or catching the long-backed *vâlai* fish that play in marshy pools thronged with eels.

"The wind may disperse swarms of bees clustering against sugar canes and tumble their hives into the ponds—which will then become sticky with bees and honey. Our weary companion, to quench her unbearable thirst, might drink from the cup of her hands this insect-polluted water.

"The peasants, pulling up weeds, will have thrown watercress taken from the streams into ditches around the fields. In the cress's damp green coolness insects of all colors may be sleeping, drunk with the flower pollen they have devoured. Unwittingly your feet may crush them as you walk.* But should you then decide to follow the embankment of the canals, you may walk on the crabs and snails and cause horrible suffering.

"The best way is one that wanders through the fields and through the forest. Friend, you wear the curly lock of hair on your head that tells me you come of a good family: think over all I have said, and try to avoid these dangers while you are traveling with this beautiful girl."

When she had finished speaking, the venerable Kavundi took up her begging bowl and the knitted bag she carried on her back. Holding the monk's fan of peacock feathers, she invoked the gods, asking that the five sacred words** might be their guide on the way. Then Kavundi, unrivaled for her experience and her merits, accompanied the young pair on their adventurous journey.

Neither angry Saturn, nor the comets wandering in the sky, nor brilliant Venus whose descent toward the southern star is a sign of drought, can perturb the river Kâverî, born of a thunderbolt in the wind-swept, rain-blessed mountains of Coorg. Spreading prosperity wherever she passes, she runs toward the swelling tide that brings into her bed the treasures of the sea. When some obstacle appears in her path, the river leaps with a deep sound in the brisk swiftness of her youthful spate. Her roar covers the noise of buckets and water-locks, the

---

* Nonviolence is one of the main virtues for the Jains; to kill an insect is a serious fault.

** The sacred word of five syllables of the Jains is *a-si-a-u-sa*, standing for *Arhat, Siddha, Âchârya, Upâdhyâya,* and *Sâdhu,* the five *parameshthins* (stages of perfection).

squeak of the balancing-poles of wells, the rustle of palm-leaf baskets used to water the fields.

In the deep forest, where lotuses raised their heavy heads above the marsh encircled with fields of sugar cane, the travelers could hear a distant clamor as if the armies of two rival kings were fighting. This uproar was made by the shrilling of insects and the cries of water-fowl, shrieking cranes, red-footed geese and green-footed herons, flying birds, and water birds of many kinds. In the damp fallow lands buffaloes ran wild, their scanty hair plastered with mud, their eyes red. They rubbed their backs against the stacks to break the long straw withes so that the grain would fall. The broken ears of rice resembled fly-whisks made of the hair of the river's gray yaks.

Field laborers, their arms blackened by exposure, came running with the farm owners. Their shouts could be heard from a distance. The travelers could also hear the simple melodies of lowborn women singing in drunken voices, their fish-shaped eyes casting lewd glances as they stood in alluring poses and cried obscene remarks to passers-by. Their broad shoulders and large breasts were soiled with mud. Having cast away the flowers from their hair, they were sticking the tender sprouts of the new rice into the water-soaked ground. These graceful and daring figures seemed like bronze statues sprung from the mire of the fields. Then the pious hymns sung by the honest ploughmen were heard. They walked behind their sharp ploughs, which ripped open the soil. They adorned the furrows with garlands of rice ears, with lotuses and glazed *arugu* grass.

From afar the travelers could hear the cowherds' threshing songs as their herds trampled the harvest to separate the grain from the straw; and the cheers of those who were listening to mud-soiled drums played by vigorous young minstrels. Listening to all these sounds along the river bank, Kannaki and Kôvalan relaxed and forgot their weariness.

Everywhere along the path they could see the smoke of offerings that priests were sacrificing in the fires of altars. The smoke seemed to cling to the roofs of the rich and the homes of the high priests, as the rain-laden clouds attracted to the hills hang on their slopes as fog. The peace of this country was the gift of the Chôla ruler, from whose chariot flies the dread tiger standard, emblem of his prowess.

Later the travelers could see ancient and wealthy villages inhabited by the powerful Kâverî's descendants, who are kind to the poor and helpful to their kin. On their constant labor the prosperity of the realm is founded.

They visited other regions with sparse hamlets, where thick smoke arose from the raw sugar melting on stoves erected near the stacks. The smoke formed a compact cloud clinging to these mountainlike stacks. But they could not walk more than four leagues a day.

After a few days they arrived at the famous city of Shrîrangam, where the river suddenly disappears. Built near the garden of heaven, the city was a place of delight, fragrant with the odor of the rarest flowers. On all sides were gardens thronged with tall trees and bordered by windbreaks of bamboos swaying gracefully in the breeze.

There they met a wandering monk known for his eloquence and his learned discourses on the sacred law that the Great Teacher once revealed to the world. He too was traveling from Puhâr, where he had taught near the polished stone erected by the Aryas in the heart of the city.

Kavundi sensed the saint's approach. She lay down on the path at his feet. Her companions did likewise, saying, "May we be free from sin." The saintly man knew the past, the present, and the future. He saw fate leading them on their last pilgrimage; yet he felt no sadness, for his mind dwelt far beyond the worlds where love and hate abide.

He spoke to them:

"Illustrious Kavundi! You know that no one ever stopped the course of destiny. No one can fail to reap the harvest grown from the seeds of his actions. Each deed brings forth its leaves and its flowers. In this body, life is like the flame of a lamp that a desert wind may suddenly blow out. Our Teacher, who knows all, is the incarnation of Dharma, the Eternal Law. He stands beyond understanding. He alone is our friend, the great lord of wisdom, the instrument of salvation, the all-powerful god, the support of the Law. He is virtue itself, the spirit of truth, pure, ancient, and wise, victorious over anger. He is the king of paradise, the lord who grants the pleasures of heaven. He is the source of all merit, the light that shines in the high spheres. He is true and humble. Wandering at his whim, he is the source of life, the powerful yogi, immense, miraculous, the seer who dwells in all, the supreme sovereign whose form is the nature of the entire universe. All honors go to him, fount of all prosperity, master of the sacred sciences. He is the source of charity, a divinity endowed with the eight sublime powers: [boundless knowledge, limitless vision, limitless strength, limitless happiness, existence beyond name, space and time, indestructibility]. He is the indivisible, the primordial substance, the cosmic quiddity to which the three sacred scriptures of the Jains bear witness. He is

62

the light that dispels ignorance. No spirit can escape from its prison of flesh without having attained the sublime vision of the truth revealed to us by him whose praise I sing today."

When she had listened to the inspired message of the wandering monk, the austere Kavundi, joining her hands on her forehead, made a new vow:

"My ears shall be closed to all words save the words of wisdom revealed by him who conquered man's three enemies: desire, anger, error. My tongue shall not call on other names than the thousand and eight names of him who defeated Eros. My eyes shall contemplate only the feet of him who could master the power of the five senses. My superfluous and vain body shall not seek rest upon the earth except in the presence of him whom superhuman virtue and grace adorn. My hands shall be clasped with respect only before him who mastered wisdom and who explained the Law to the adepts. My head shall be adorned with no other flower than the lotus-feet of the saint who walks upon flowers. Henceforth my mind shall recall no other memory than the revealed words of the God whose substance is eternal joy."

Having listened with favor to this eulogy, the wandering monk left the ground and rose to a height of two cubits. From there he blessed Kavundi, saying, "May the bonds that have fastened the chain of your lives be loosened." Then he went away by the heavenly path while the travelers were praying, "May we be freed of all bonds."

At the pier they took a ferry. Clouds, heralds of rains, were gathering above the river's course. The saint and the young couple crossed the holy waters and reached the majestic temples that stood on the southern bank. There they took a few days' rest in a quiet grove carpeted with flowers.

Shortly after they arrived, a young swain, repeating commonplace compliments to the girl of his fancy, entered the flowery garden. Curious to know the origins of Kannaki and Kôvalan, who so resembled Kâma [Love] and his mistress Rati [Desire], the couple approached Kavundi and the young man asked her:

"Who are these young people following you in your travels?"

Kavundi answered gently:

"They are just my children, human beings. Leave them in peace. They are weary after a long journey."

The visitors giggled:

"Saintly woman, you who seem to know the holy scriptures so well, did you ever notice that children of one bed behave like man and wife?"

Kannaki shut her ears to these improper words, and stood trembling near her husband. But Kavundi, rich in the powers she had gained through her penance, cursed the two intruders:

"May you henceforth be two jackals roaming in the thorny jungles."

This curse had come from a great saint: soon Kôvalan and his wife could hear the howl of two jackals. Trembling with fear, they said:

"Truly those who leave the path of virtue are apt to speak indecently. Yet do you not think, great saint, that these youngsters did not fully realize what they were saying? Tell us when these unfortunates, who misbehaved in your saintly presence, may be freed from your curse?"

The saint answered:

"Those to whom it happens that they fall into low forms of life because of evil deeds must wander in pain for one year. Till then they shall live in the thick forest under the walls of Uraiyûr's fortress. After that they will recover their previous appearance."

Once the duration of the curse had been pronounced, the saintly Kavundi, taking Kôvalan and his wife with her, entered the town of Uraiyûr, which people also call Vâranam, the city of the elephant. There once long ago a hen, armored only by her feathers, defeated in single combat a rogue elephant whose ears were bigger than the baskets used for winnowing.

❧❧ BOOK TWO ❧❧

Madurai

CANTO ELEVEN

The Forest

Kâdukânkâdai

In the deep shade of an *ashoka* tree that inclined its flower-laden branches toward him, the old god Arivan —born of himself and more splendid than the sun rising in the east—was reclining. Above him a triple parasol resembled three moons sheltering one another. The saint Kavundi first kneeled at his feet, then arose and expounded words of wisdom and charity that the holy monk, in olden times, had spoken before the sages assembled near a temple of the young god Murugan in the gardens of the venerable city of Arangam.

The travelers spent the whole day in their place of repose. But, anxious to start toward the south, they left Vâranam before the next dawn, when the eastern sky was still blushing at the sight of the sun. Passing through a fertile country, they came to a pillared hall surrounded by trees and gardens. In all directions they could see rich rice fields scattered between shining sheets of water. And all around them tender crops were undulating in the breeze.

They met a most venerable Brahmin, prone to sing the praises of the Pândya king—ruler over the central Tamil kingdom—whose noble name has remained ever unsullied:

"May the great king live forever, protecting the whole earth for all ages to come. Long live our Tennavan, ruler of the southern lands, to which he annexed the Ganges and the northern Himalaya. To show his valor to other monarchs, he hurled his spear against the furious sea, which, in its rage, devoured the river Pahruli and the land of the Kumari together with its vast circle of mountains.

"Long live the king who, on his brilliant chest, wears the glorious garland of the King of Heaven, and has added many a noble deed to those accomplished in the past by the princes of the Moon's dynasty.

"Long live our king! For, when the clouds refused to give their rain to the suffering land, he broke the ring shining on Indra's crown and made all the clouds prisoners, that the country might prosper and rich crops be secured."

Kôvalan asked him:

"Which is your native land, and what are you doing in this country?"

The Brahmin answered with unshakable pride:

"I am a citizen of Mânkâdu, in the country beyond the eastern hills. I came here to fulfill a vow and to see, in the temple standing on the island that separates the fierce flow of the Kâverî into two streams, the glorious image of Vishnu, here worshiped while he rests, with the goddess Fortune against his heart, on the huge hundred-headed serpent like a dark cloud asleep on the polar mountain. I walked for many days in order to contemplate the beauty of this red-eyed god, holding in his hand the lotus, the discus that kills all his opponents, and the conch as white as milk. Clad in yellow, he wears on his broad chest a wreath of white flowers. He dwells on the hill of Venkata, whence many streams of crystal water spring.

"The dark-blue god, holding discus and conch, is decked with colorful garlands. He resembles a majestic rainbow-hued cloud bejeweled with dazzling thunderbolts, of which one side flames under the burning sun, the other is cooled by the light of the moon. Since I could see, for the joy of my eyes, the glory of the Pândya king, I stayed here blessing the country. That is the tale of my journey."

After listening further to the priest, who had performed many sacrifices in accordance with Vedic rites, Kôvalan asked:

"Best of Brahmins, tell us the road to take to Madurai."

The Brahmin answered:

"The season in which you are traveling with your wife is one when mountains and forests have lost life and color and seem a desert waste. King Sun, and Spring his minister, have become such misers that they permit only scanty rains on the earth. The roads' smooth surfaces have been worn away: sharp stones wound weary travelers. The vast fields, parched with drought, suggest a kingdom whose ruler, at the instigation of corrupt ministers, has gone astray from the path of duty.

"During the journey, you will have to climb over rocks and hills; you will have to traverse dangerous mirages, cross dams crumbling under the thrust of swollen lakes, until, near an inland sea, you reach the

71

town of Kodumbai, where the road divides into three, like the fierce trident of the god who wears the crescent moon on his brow.

"Should you decide to take the road that goes toward the right, you will pass a *kadamba* with wide-spreading branches, then, near a dead tree, you will see a cleft *vâhai*, withered bamboos, and an old *maral*, dry and black, its trunk split up by crevices. Your gaze will wander on to drought-parched jungles where forlorn deer search vainly for a pond. You will see the shelters of the cruel hunters before you reach, at last, the celebrated hill of the Pândyas that people call *shirumalai*, the little hill, among fields of wild rice, sugar cane, ripe millet, and other rich crops that grow only in fertile soil. That region produces garlic, saffron, and lovely *kavalai* creepers. The best plantains, areca nuts, coconuts in clusters, mangoes, and cucumbers also grow there. Leaving the hill on your right, you will reach the great city of Madurai.

"Should you prefer the left-hand road, you will cross some lowlands with fields and shady groves full of flowers, interspersed with rocks and jungles spreading as far as the eye can see. There the country is alive with the constant murmur of beetles and insects that seem to be humming in the mode called *shevvali*. Nearer to Madurai, you will reach a hill sacred to Lord Vishnu, through which a dark passage leads to a world where all illusions are destroyed. There will appear before you three miraculous lakes, whose virtues are sung even by the gods — called the Thicket-of-Arrows, the Fulfiller-of-Fate, and the Attainer-of-Desires. If you bathe in the Thicket-of-Arrows, you gain knowledge of the language revealed in ancient times by the King of Heaven. Should you immerse yourself in the Fulfiller-of-Fate, you will recall all the deeds of past lives, which are the sources of our present ones. If you enter the cool waters of the Attainer-of-Desires, any wish you may make will be at once fulfilled.

"Should you wish to enter the cave, you should first go to pray to the god of the hill, meditate on his lotus feet, then walk three times around the mountain.

"Near the sacred river Shilâmbaru, which ploughs its furrow through the earth near a blossoming *kôngu* that scatters its petals, you will meet a *yakshinî* nymph, fairer than a golden liana, more dazzling than the lightning-flash, with hair darker than rain clouds. High near her shoulders she wears notched gold armlets. Of all the passers-by she asks riddles:

"'Tell me, what is the source of happiness in this world and in the world beyond? What eternal life is not of this world nor of the world beyond? I live on this hill and my name is Varôttamâ; I will become the bondmaid of those who can answer my queries. Wise travelers, if you can give the right answers, I will unlock for you the entrance to the nether world, where you will see several passages closed by doors and then a double gate. Beyond the gate a virgin will appear, frail as a liana, precious and rare as a picture. She will ask you, "What is the meaning of eternal life?" If you know the answer, you may make three wishes, one of which shall be fulfilled. Should you remain silent, no harm shall come to you. Go your way! I give you my help and my support.'

"The nymph leads those travelers who can answer to the three ponds, then she vanishes. After bathing, one should make three wishes, and then sit and meditate, uttering with fervor the two sacred mantras of Shiva and Vishnu, as revealed in the scriptures, which have five or eight syllables. Thus one gains with great ease such celestial blessings as the most severe penance could hardly, in this life, obtain.

"Those who do not seek worldly gain may simply meditate on the lotus feet of the god who resides on the hill. Soon they have a vision, and can see his standard, bearing a black eagle. He who obtains this rare vision is liberated forever from the cycle of lives. So go now to Madurai, the glorious Pândya capital, and rejoice at the thought of the vision you may have on the way!

"Should you not like either of the two roads I have mentioned, there remains the last one, which wanders through clean villages nestling among the honey groves, and traverses a thorny jungle. Ahead stands a genie who does no harm to travelers: he will speak gently and let you go on. Once you pass him, the road to Madurai is open before you. So start now, while I go to worship the footprints of the god who crossed the universe with but three strides."

Having listened to the Brahmin's description of the roads, the saintly Kavundi replied:

"O priest versed in the four *Vedas* and employed in good deeds! We have no desire to enter the subterranean road. The doctrine revealed by Indra, who lives longer than other gods, is part of our sacred books. When we wish to know some event in our past lives, it is easier for us to look for its effect in present happenings. Is there anything that cannot be accomplished by a man who seeks the truth and longs only for charity? Go on your pilgrimage in search of any god you choose; as for us, we shall follow our path."

Having given to the Brahmin the answers he deserved, she spent the evening taking her rest with Kôvalan, noble of soul, who now never strayed from the path of duty. The next morning they resumed their journey.

One day, while the wise Kavundi and dark-eyed Kannaki were resting near the road, Kôvalan saw a narrow path leading away from the main thoroughfare. He followed it and found a lake. He came down to its shore to quench his thirst. There a forest nymph, who, stung by lust, had taken the form of Vasanta-mâlâ, the maid of Mâdhavi, drew near, hoping that Kôvalan would satisfy her lewd longings. Shedding deceitful tears, she cast herself down at his feet, and, trembling like a creeper, said to him:

"Mâdhavi told me, 'There was nothing improper in what I wrote on the wreath of flowers. You must have told some lie that caused Kôvalan to be harsh and cruel to me.' Then she fainted away under the burden of her grief. When she regained consciousness, she told me: 'The worst profession is that of a courtesan. Learned and pious people avoid her as they would a diseased person; those who prefer good to evil turn away from her path.' My mistress wept and lamented. Pearl-like tears fell from her soft, hazy eyes. She suddenly tore her splendid pearl necklace to pieces and let the pearls scatter. Then she sent me away. I met some travelers setting out for Madurai, the ancient city, and they spoke of you. So I joined them and came with their caravan. Generous soul, what will you do to save me from my great distress?"

Warned by the learned Brahmin of the danger from charming nymphs who haunt these lonely woods, Kôvalan started to murmur the sacred words that dispel all weird charms: he uttered the invocation to the goddess who rides a deer. As soon as she heard his prayers, the nymph ran away, confessing:

"I am a spirit of the woods who attempted to lead you astray. Do not mention my evil deed to your good wife, more beautiful than a peacock, or to the saint, but go your way."

Finding a green lotus leaf, Kôvalan brought water in it to the fatigued women, and quenched their thirst. Seeing that it was not possible to walk at that hour under the burning sun, Kôvalan and frail Kannaki, with the curved anklets at her feet, walked up to a garden in bloom, where they could see flowers of *kurava, kadamba, kôngu,* and *vengai.* There they found a temple, dedicated to Kâlî the goddess of Death, whose eyes are tongues of fire and who lives in heaven, worshiped by all the gods. In this place that the rains never bless, bandits dwelt who were skilled in handling fearful bows and arrows and lived by despoiling travelers of all their possessions. As if guided by Yama, the king of Hades, they raided neighboring countries, brandishing their bows. The goddess gave them victory and expected a bloody sacrifice as a reward for her favor.

꙰꙰ CANTO TWELVE ꙰꙰

Songs of the Hunters

Vettuvavari

The Sun ceaselessly poured down its burning rays that made all travel an ordeal. Fragrant-haired Kannaki's tender feet were blistered: she gave way to tears and moans. They stopped near a lonely village in which was the temple of Aiyai, the goddess of hunters.

76

Shâlini was born in the fierce Maravar tribe, whose warriors have never laid down their arms. One day, possessed by a genie, she began to dance. Her hair stood on her head; her hands were flung up in wild fervor. The forest folk looked at her with awe and stupefaction. She danced in the *Manram*, the common eating ground, in the very center of the Eiynars' stronghold, protected from all attacks by thorny hedges. She spoke, and her words seemed to echo the inner urge of all who heard her:

"The herds prosper in all enemy villages, while the communal storehouses of the Eiynars appear empty. Have the fierce hunters of the Maravar tribe lost their strength and courage? They follow after virtues that are good for peasants, and forget the glorious art of stripping travelers of their wealth. When the goddess who rides a stag is starved of offerings, she does not send her servant, Victory, to guide warriors' arrows to their mark. For the brave Maravars, virtue lies in the heartlessness of plunder. If you seek happiness, do your duty. Go! Get drunk on strong wine and bring the goddess her dues."

The sons of the ancient Eiynar tribe prefer a glorious death on the field of battle to a village funeral pyre. From time immemorial the goddess had chosen to become incarnate in a virgin of that courageous tribe. In her short hair, tied in a tuft, there appeared silvery snakes entwined round the white crescent-shaped tusk of a boar that had destroyed all the tender plants in well-kept enemy gardens. Her necklace was made of the teeth of a lusty tiger. Her short skirt was a leopard's hide with the spots and stripes on the outside. In her hand she carried a bow of well-seasoned wood. She rode a stag with black antlers. Eiynar women came to lay at her feet dolls, parrots, soft-feathered cockerels, blue peacocks, and playing balls and black beans for divination.

They followed her, carrying powders, fragrant unguents, boiled grain, pastries of sesamum seeds, rice cooked with meat, flowers, incense, and perfumes, while she was led to the temple of Anangu, who feasts on cruel sacrifices and gives victory in return. There one could hear the deep sound of the drums used in the armed exploits of the dacoits, and the trumpets that had often given the signal for plunder, mixed with the music of sacred bells and songs.

The virgin prostrated herself before the goddess who rides a stag. Suddenly she became inspired. Looking at Kannaki, who was standing near her husband on her tiny feet bruised by the journey, she cried:

"She has come, the princes of the Kongunâdu, the Tamils of the north, the sovereign of the western hills, the queen of the southern Tamil land! She is the flower of virtue, a matchless jewel crowning the Earth."

Kannaki, shyly hiding behind her husband's broad shoulders, smiled at such fancies. She thought:

"This soothsayer speaks out of ignorance."

Shâlini, now transformed into an apparition of the consort of Shiva, came nearer. The crescent moon shone in her matted tresses. The eye in the center of her forehead gazed unblinking. Her lips were blood-red; her teeth shone. Her neck seemed black with poison. Vâsuki, the serpent whose rage is never satiated, was coiled round her loins. She held the bow of the northern mountain. The skin of a venomous snake covered her breasts. An elephant's hide hung from her shoulders, that of a lion formed her skirt. She brandished a blazing trident in her hand. A heavy circlet adorned her left ankle. Small bells tied to her foot seemed to foretell a victory. Deft in swordplay, the goddess stood over a black genie with two broadshouldered torsos. Worshiped by all the gods, she was called the virgin, the white one, the end of life. Younger sister of Vishnu the all-pervader, she was blue. Victorious in all battles, bearing high her fearful axe, she was truly Durgâ the goddess beyond reach. Born of a stag, she was both Lakshmî, Fortune, and Sarasvatî, Knowledge—the most valuable gifts that may be sought. Ever virgin, she was ever young. Before her, Vishnu and Brahmâ bowed with humility. All who saw her could attest that the form and the appearance of Shâlini, possessed by the goddess, was prodigious.

THE GLORY OF THE SHRINE

Uraippâttumadai

Cinnamon and sweet *narandai* grew before the altar where sacrifices are offered to the goddess who sits at the side of the three-eyed god Shiva. Here and there were groves of *sâl* and sandal, which, like the mango trees, had put on their richest foliage. Before the shrine of the goddess, whose hair is adorned with the moon, the kinos poured down a rain of golden petals. Red cottonwood trees seemed crushed under their rich burden of flowering branches. *Pongamias* scattered their white blossoms on the ground. Before the sanctuary of Vishnu's young sister, the *kadamba*, the bignonias, the *punnai, kuravu* the fragrant verbena, and *kôngu* the red *hopea*, were in bloom. The soft murmur of swarms of bees on the branches resembled the gentle sound of a lute.

IN PRAISE OF SHALINI

The merits of the girl with the gold ornaments
  are boundless.
Her form and her vesture are those
of the goddess of victory.

The only name that stands for unsullied courage
is the name of the hunters' tribe.
There the maiden with the gold anklets was born.

The virtues of the girl with the golden ornaments
   are boundless.
Her pubis is like a cobra's hood.
She wears the ornaments of Aiyai, goddess of Death.
Born in the glorious tribe of the Eiynars,
who shoot their deadly arrows with unrivaled skill,
this girl, her ankles laden with most splendid circlets,
seems to be possessed of all the attributes
of that goddess one sees at dusk crossing the path,
riding a stag more swift than lightning.
The lovely maiden with the rich anklets
was born in the fierce Eiynar tribe,
whose bows are made of strong bamboo.

OTHER HYMNS TO SHALINI

A Description of the Goddess Durgâ

Before you the gods humbly bow.
Your arm has never known defeat.
You are the wisdom of the Book of Books.
How came you to appear,
robed in a tiger skin, standing
on the black head of a wild buffalo,
with an elephant's tough hide for your cloak?

You shine as a flame
in the heart of Vishnu, who destroys all pain,
in the heart of Shiva, the destroyer of the world,
in the heart of Brahmâ, lord of vastness.
You came wandering on a stag

80

that proudly bears black antlers.
You hold in your bracelet-laden hands
a sword dripping with blood
after you killed the buffalo demon.

The *Vedas* sing your praises, for you are
consort of him who bears the Ganges,
a third eye gazing from his brow.
Why must you stand on a fierce lion
whose eyes shoot darts of flame,
holding in your frail lotus hand
a discus and a conch?

Wreathed with venomous datura,
a scarf of basil leaves on her shoulder,
the chosen virgin dances for the god's delight,
scattering fear among the demon's hosts.

OTHER HYMNS

With belt and bangles all of gold,
the goddess danced the *marakkâl*, the stilt-dance,
with sword in hand, defeating
perfidious demons armed with spears.
One heard the tinkle of her anklets
filled with golden chips.
With sword in hand, she danced the stilt-dance
to defeat perfidious genii armed with spears.
Her face was the color of the pepper blossom.
The gods praised the goddess
and showered a rain of fragrant flowers upon her.

When a proud warrior, keen to win
the victor's scarlet garland of ixora,
leaves his humble hamlet, and, braving all risks,

seizes the cattle of the enemy,
he calls for aid upon the goddess
who destroys all with her glittering sword.
Then the forest's king-crow, cawing
his cry of ill omen, falls from the sky
over the enemy villages.

When the woman who sells palm wine
will no longer serve the too-indebted hunter,
he consults the flight of the birds
and, seizing his bow, sets off in search
of the herds of his enemy.
Then the goddess spreads her conquering standard,
on which a lion stands,
and she walks ahead of the hunter's bow.

CHANT

Maiden with lovely teeth!
Look at the vast herd of cattle
captured by our elders;
today this booty fills the courtyards
of our famous ironsmiths,
our drummers, and our bards
adept at playing on the harp,
with whom the warriors have shared it.

Maiden with lovely teeth!
Look at the herds our elders have plundered,
destroying the herdsmen who should have guarded them.
Today they crowd the yards of our palm-wine sellers,
of our mysterious spies who hide in the forests,
and of our learned magicians
who interpret the strange flight of the birds.

Maiden! Your eyes are dark with collyrium.
Your skin has the color of the pepper blossom.

Look at the herds our elders have captured,
bringing untold hardship to the enemy farms.
Today they crowd the yards of the heartless Eiynars,
men with gray mustaches, coarse in their speech,
who live beside their old and faithful wives.

MINOR HYMNS

Turaippâttumadai

We worship your feet! At sight of them
the sages and the gods, who follow the wandering sun,
forget the hardships of the way.
Accept the blood that flows from our severed young heads,
the price of a victory you granted
to the powerful and valiant Eiynars.

We worship the lotus of your feet,
God darker than the blue sapphire!
Before you all the gods, led by Indra their king,
come to bow with humble respect.
Accept the blood and flesh we offer you,
in thanks for the great victories
you showered on the Eiynars
when they adventured out on raids
to seize vast herds of cattle.

Virgin goddess! Accept our blood, our sacrifice
performed before your altar
in fulfillment of the Eiynars' vow.
The tigerish warriors lie prostrate now
before the lotus of your feet.
Soon they shall start, some somber night,

sounding their clear small *tudi* drums,
their deep-voiced *parai*, drums of war,
and flutes that rip apart
the starry vault of night.

THE SACRIFICE

O source of peace! Goddess of destiny!
Blue goddess, wearing in your hair
the red-eyed serpent and the crescent moon,
accept the offerings of the Eiynars,
whose bows are strong and arrows sharp.
To recompense our sacrifice
send many a traveler within our reach
that our wealth may grow immense.

All the gods worship you.
You drank the nectar, and yet you died,
rendered immortal by the fatal brew
no god dared touch. Come!
Feast on the offerings the hard-hearted Eiynars
bring to you. Then, when the world's asleep,
we'll raid some far-off farms, beating our drums
before the plundering begins.

You shower your blessings on the world,
shattering with a stroke of your foot
that fearful and Earth-crushing wheel
your uncle launched upon its deadly course,*

---

* King Kamsa sent a demon *(asura)* in the shape of a wheel that
destroyed everything in its path. The child Krishna stopped it
and broke it with his foot.

uprooted too the twin trees in the fields,*
forcing your passage in between.
Accept these sacrifices, overdue,
offered to you by the cruel Eiynars,
who live by plundering of others' wealth
and carry, everywhere they go,
a tale of hunger, of despair and death.

INVOCATION

Let the Pândya, anxious to win in the battle
against the enemy armies' powerful array,
place on his crown the red ixora flower,
symbol of successful conquest. May we
be led to victory by the mighty god
of Mount Podiyil, where resides,
equal to Brahmâ, the sage Agastya, who revealed
the Book of Wisdom to the world.

꒞ CANTO THIRTEEN ꒞

The Neighborhood of Madurai

Purancêriiruttakâdai

After Shâlini the dancer had gone, Kôvalan bowed before
the saint and said:
    "This young girl can no longer bear the fierceness of
the burning sun. Her tender feet cannot endure the stones.

---

* An allusion to two celestial musicians changed into trees, which
  the child Krishna uprooted, thus liberating them.

This land belongs to the Pândya monarch. The story of his virtues has spread to the four corners of the world. Here the savage bear does not dare to crush the busy hives, the striped tiger is the friend of the swift deer. Snakes, ghosts, and crocodiles, waiting for their prey, dare not touch innocent wayfarers. Therefore, instead of traveling by day, let us cross the forest by night, by the light of the moon, gentle to all creatures. We need fear no danger."

The saint gladly agreed to this wise suggestion. They waited for the sun to set, as courtiers wait for a tyrant to retire. The Moon, ancestor of the Pândya kings, soon appeared with its train of stars, and dispensed the milk of its rays. Before falling asleep with a sigh of relief, the Earth plaintively said:

"Up to this late hour, dots of sandal paste have not, like a necklace of stars, stained the breasts of this fair girl. Her hair has not been studded with lilies and other blossoms pouring forth their sweet pollen. Her lithe body, tender as a flower bud, is not adorned with wreaths of rare petals. A southern breeze, born in the Malayan hills, and grown up in the town of Madurai, where it has danced over the tongues of poets, seems to call her and to caress her body tenderly. To soothe her, the Spring moon pours down its abundant milky rays."

To his young wife, weary after the long journey, Kôvalan said:

"Tonight we shall see striped tigers crossing our path, we shall hear the hooting of owls, the grunts of bears, and the crash of thunder. You must not be afraid."

He drew over his shoulder her graceful arm loaded with gold bracelets. Then they set off through the forest, piously listening to the words of wisdom spoken by the saintly Kavundi, who was learned in all things divine,

86

until a bird, hidden in the sun-dried bamboo forest, called to tell them that dawn was at hand.

Soon they reached a large village inhabited by Brahmins. These Brahmins wore the sacred thread, but were addicted to music and dancing. For this sin they had lost their rank. Kôvalan left his frail wife and the saint in a secure and sheltered place, and, after slipping through hedges of thorny bush, he walked along the road in search of clean water for their morning ablutions. He thought of the journey through fearful forests that he had so lightly undertaken with a frail woman. He sighed like a goldsmith's bellows and felt a pain so keen it seemed as if a fatal wound had been dealt his soul.

Now it happened that a young priest from Puhâr named Kaushikan had been dispatched into the forest by Mâdhavi to search for Kôvalan. But he did not recognize him at first, so changed was Kôvalan's appearance by sadness, and the young Brahmin went on talking to the tree under which he was resting:

"O tree so dear to Mâdhavi, you cast away all your flowers, unable to bear the hardship of this deathly season. In your distress you resemble Mâdhavi of the long dark eyes, overwhelmed by fearful sorrow. She cannot bear to live away from Kôvalan."

Kôvalan overheard the Brahmin Kaushikan, and called:

"Where have you come from?"

Young Kaushikan approached, and joyfully exclaimed:

"My worries are ended, for I have met you at last!" He told Kôvalan the news of Puhâr. His wealthy father and his aged mother looked like dried-up snakes that have lost the jewels from their brows. All his relatives and friends seemed drowned in oceans of sorrow, as if their minds had been withdrawn from their bodies. His servants had gone in all directions in search of him, hoping to bring him home. The whole of the great city of Puhâr had lost its head, and was lamenting like Ayodhyâ when the great hero Râma left to lead the life of a recluse in the forest, and said: "A kingdom is not worth the great sin of disobedience." Mâdhavi, when she heard the news from a report of Vasanta-mâlâ, had lost her color and turned green. She had fainted on her precious bed in the love-chamber of her rich mansion. Kaushikan said: "Grieved at the sight of her sorrow, I attempted to console her. In her anguish she cried: 'Look at me, prostrate at your feet! Put an end to my suffering!' With her graceful hand she wrote a message and handed it to me, saying: 'Go! Take this sealed palm leaf to him who is dearer to me than my own eyes.'" The priest, leaving altar and sacrifice, had wandered about the country carrying the letter with him.

Kaushikan spoke with emotion, and placed in Kôvalan's hands the leaf that, in her grief, lianalike Mâdhavi, her long hair adorned with flowers, had entrusted to him. The mere sight of the seal reminded Kôvalan of the sweet scent of her tresses, burnished with fragrant oil, when he had been her lover. He paused before breaking the ring; then opened the palm leaf and read:

"Lord of my life! I lie prostrate at your feet. Forgive me for being importunate. What was my fault that you were led to depart one dark night with your most noble wife, without telling your good parents? I am unable to understand, and my heart is broken. Help me, noble and sincere heart! And bless me with wisdom."

Having read her message, Kôvalan thought, "She did no wrong. I alone am to blame." He gave back the letter to Kaushikan, for it would explain his sudden departure, and said:

"The contents of this sealed palm leaf must be read by my wise parents. I bow before their lotus feet. Go, young Kaushikan! Bring this letter to them to relieve their anxiety and free them from anguish."

After his return to the shelter where the saintly Kavundi and his innocent bride were waiting for him, Kôvalan met some wandering minstrels who were singing a hymn depicting the war-dance of the fierce Durgâ, the goddess beyond reach. He borrowed a lute called *shengôtti*, and, to adjust its scale *(shentiram)*, he slid the gut-string knots on the curved arm *(tantri-karam)*. He carefully adjusted the frets along the finger board *(parru)*, then tuned the strings, beginning with the fourth and ending with the third. He then verified the tuning of the mode *(âshânriram)* that had seven notes in its descending scale and but five in ascent *(pâtarpâni)*—a mode that, sacred to the goddess Durgâ, should be played with three variations *(tânam)*.

After singing hymns with the rustic bards, Kôvalan asked them the distance to Madurai. They answered:

"Do you not feel the southern breeze blowing from the city and bringing us the mixed fragrance of sacred black *akil* and sandalwood? This breeze comes here laden with the odors of saffron, chives, sandal paste, and musk. On its way it may have wandered near newly opened buds of sweet water lilies pouring out their abundant pollen; or trailed among champaks in bloom, or lost its way in groves of jasmine and *mâdhavi*, or caressed the buds of garden *mullai*. It brings us a smell of good food, for it went through the fumes of big bazaars, where pancakes are fried in countless little stalls. It brings with it a heavy odor from the terraces where men and women crowd close together. It is thick with the smoke of sacrifices and many other pleasing smells. It blows through the palace of the great Pândya king, who wears on his broad chest a chain of gold that the king of the gods once gave him. This breeze that carries strange and varied smells about the country is very different from the other wind that blows from the Podiyil hill, whose glory was sung by the faultless tongues of the Tamil bards. The wealthy city is not far off, and you need have no fear. Even if you go there alone, you will meet no danger on your way."

Accompanied by the saint, famous for her virtues, Kôvalan and Kannaki completed the last night of their journey. Toward morning they heard, like distant thunder, the sound of drums being beaten in Shiva's great temple and in the sanctuaries of all the other gods, as well as in the great palace of the famous king whose renown has traveled to the ends of the world. They could hear the *Vedas* being chanted by the learned Brahmins and the prayers being recited by the monks, filling the morning air with their holy murmur. They could hear the roll of victory drums *(mulavu)*, which are beaten daily in honor of the warriors, armed with swords, who never come back from the battlefield except as victors. They could also hear trumpeting elephants, captured on the field of battle, and the cries of wild tuskers caught in the deep forests, the neighing of horses in their stalls, the noise of *kinai*, the small drums used to accompany dancers practicing at dawn, and many vague sounds arising from the city, which recalled the murmur of a perfidious ocean. To the tired travelers these sounds seemed friendly calls of welcome, and made them forget the hardships experienced on the way.

The Vaigai (or Madurai) River, daughter of the Sky, wanders ever on the tongues of poets, who sing the generous gifts she bestows on the land she has blessed. Most cherished possession of the Pândya kingdom, she resembles a noble and respected maiden. Her dress is woven of all the flowers that fall from the date tree, the *vakulam*, the kino, the white *kadamba*, the gamboge, the *tilak*, the jasmine, the myrobalan, the pear tree, the great champak, and the saffron plant. The broad belt she wears low around her hips is adorned with lovely flowers of *kuruku* and golden jasmine, mixed with the *mushundai's* thick lianas, the wild jasmine, the convolvulus, the bamboo, the volubilis, the *pidavam*, and Arabian jasmine. The sandbanks, edged by trees in blossom, are her youthful breasts. Her red lips are the trees that spread their red petals along the shore. Her lovely teeth are wild jasmine buds floating in the stream. Her long eyes are the carp, which playing in the water, appear and vanish like a wink. Her tresses are the flowing waters filled with petals.

As if she knew the sad fate that lay in store for young Kannaki, the Vaigai had put on her best veil made of precious flowers, and could not hold back the tears that filled her eyes. After passing along narrow paths through the woods, Kannaki and Kôvalan reached the bank of the river. Both cried out in wonder:

"This is not a river but a stream in blossom."

They avoided the crowded piers where the boats were moored, some shaped like horses, others like elephants or lions. With the saint, they crossed the river on a ferry and reached the southern bank near a garden fragrant with the rarest flowers. To earn some merit, they first walked, as pilgrims do, around the walls of the town where the gods dwell. They followed the ramparts, covered with thick overgrowth. At sight of them, the water lilies and the pale lotuses in the ponds seemed to shudder on their stems and shed tears as if they foresaw the tragedy awaiting them. The bees hummed a funeral dirge. The banners, reminders of former victories, floating high above the ramparts, waved in the wind like hands warning them not to approach the town.

The weary travelers entered a suburb of the old city, famed for the virtues of its citizens. Rice fields full of birds could be seen between the tall mansions. Around the large shimmering ponds were rows of bamboo huts. They took rest in a cool coconut grove where bananas and tall areca palms were growing.

✣✣ CANTO FOURTEEN ✣✣

The Sights of the City

Urkânkâdai

The sun, worshiped by the whole world, arose to the music of morning birds that dwell in suburban gardens, among shimmering ponds and fields where a rich ripe harvest waved in the wandering breeze. At sight of the sun, the lotuses opened in the lakes and pools. Through the morning haze it woke from their sleep the people of the proud city, where the Pândya king rules and whence he sets out to destroy enemies by the power of his sword. The thunder of the morning drums and the sound of the conch arose in the morning air from the sacred temples of Shiva the three-eyed, of Vishnu who displays a bird on his standard, of Baladeva holding his plough, and of young Murugan whose banner bears a cock. The chanting of prayers was heard in the homes of the priests, conversant with celestial law, and in the palace of the ever-victorious king.

Kôvalan approached Kavundi the saint, and he bowed at her feet. Clasping his hands, he said:

"O noble saint, famed for rare asceticism! I once strayed from the path of duty. Now I feel desperate when I see this frail woman who with me has scoured faraway lands over such arduous paths. I feel myself the source of all the sufferings that this flower, whom I tenderly love, has endured. May this wife of mine stay under your protection until I return from a visit to the princely merchants of this ancient city? O saint, I know that nothing untoward can happen to her while she is in your hands."

Kavundi replied:

"The merits you had stored up in previous lives are exhausted. You and the one you love must prepare for the most terrible misfortune. In this world the sages sound in vain a drum-call of warning when they say: 'Avoid the tempting path of sin, for a man shall reap what he has sown.' But those men who are weak do not listen to their advice, and when, the evil deed performed, fate claims its dues, they drown in a sea of despair born of their blindness. The saintly and the wise shed no tears when such men reap the fruits of their deeds.

"The torment of being far away from the cherished one, the desire to possess the object of love, and all the sufferings the god of Love inflicts, are known only to those who lose their self-control in the embrace of fragrant-haired women. These pains cannot even touch the sage who observes chastity. In this world, countless are the unfortunates who fall into fearful predicaments in their mad pursuit of women, of wealth, of pleasure. That is why the sages renounce all desire for worldly things. It is not starting from today but from the moment of his first creation that man has been the victim of all the traps that lust lays in his path, and must, as a consequence, undergo fearful suffering. Do you not know that Râma, who went into exile with his most faithful bride to comply with his father's wish, and who felt such unbearable pain when he was later torn away from this woman he loved, was the very father of him who revealed all wisdom to mankind? This tale comes down from the most ancient times.

"Have you not heard the story of Nala and Damayantî? Nala staked his kingdom at gambling, and lost; and he had to wander in the dense forest with the frail Damayantî, the girl he would not abandon. It was not her selfishness, nor indeed any fault of hers, that finally tore them apart, but a merciless fate that compelled him to leave his loved one in a jungle one somber night. Now tell me, was Damayantî guilty of any crime? You are more fortunate, for you are to remain beside your beautiful wife for all time to come. Do not weep! Go see Madurai, a city of great kings. Come back to us when you have discovered the new home that you are seeking."

Kôvalan entered the city through a winding passage near the huge gate where the elephants pass, waving their trunks. This passage crossed the broad moat filled with shining water, bordered by thick brushwork, forming a secure protection. Unnoticed by the Greek mercenaries, armed with swords, who kept watch at the gate, he passed the bastion, covered with junglelike overgrowth, over which the banners waved in the western wind. Suddenly he could see the splendor of the city, as if the treasure of the thousand-eyed Indra had miraculously been spread out before him.

In the streets he saw courtesans shamelessly accompanying the wealthy men who kept them toward pleasure-gardens shaded by great *maruda* trees on the dunes bordering the abundant Vaigai. There boys were playing in the water, some seated on skiffs or large houseboats, others swimming, holding on to little floats.

In the garden of the old town, common prostitutes were gracefully walking, their hair adorned with fresh jasmine, water lilies, and new lotus blossoms. They wore garlands of white jasmine and red lilies held by strings of rare pearls coming from the port of Korkai. They had rubbed their fair bodies with sandal paste from the Malayan hills.

At night the young women sat on moonlit terraces, their beds strewn with flowers. Their lovers soon made them forget the hard work of the day, till the King of the Clouds, appearing with the southern breeze, spread his scarlet veil over the city. Everywhere garlands of many hues could be admired. Clad in flowers, the ancient Madurai could boast of its riches to Indra, who with his thunderbolt had once clipped the mountains' wings.

During the rainy months, all the women of the city wore round their hips transparent veils of red silk embroidered with flowers. They adorned their hair with olive foliage, strobilanthus flowers, and red blossoms of *tâli* grown on the Shirumalai hill. They painted on their breasts a filigree of sandal paste over which their coral necklaces and long garlands of red *shengôdu* gleamed.

In the great mansions, built by renowned architects, which appeared to touch the sky, timid maidens in the cool season sat beside braseros burning incense wood; near them were their lovers, whose chests were white with sandal paste. The windows were closed by curtains of woven reeds.

In the season of dews, many women who at other times often spent the night with their lovers on the high roofs bathed in moonlight, now came up only to enjoy the soft warmth of the Sun that spread its morning rays toward the southern sky and dispersed the furry clouds. They said:

"Where is the king of the late dew of Spring? Shall he not come to see the festival of archery with which we in the Pândya capital honor Neduvêl, the cruel-hearted god of Pleasure? Shall he not come, driven by eastern winds, bringing a convoy of great ships laden with incense, silk, sandalwood, perfumes, and camphor, sent from Tondi as tribute? Where else than in the joyful town where the great Pândya reigns could we see the ruler of Spring, who inspires love? Shall he not come, brought on the desert wind that blows from the Podiyil hill over our southern land? Shall he not bring with him a rich harvest of *mâdhavi* flowers? Shall he not fill the now bleak bushlands with many-hued flowers that make the air fragrant?" Thus the women, frail as lianas, recalled the cycle of the seasons while relaxing beside their lords.

When the warm Sun, wedded to the western wind, entering the town of Madurai, causes Summer's rule to be undisputedly acknowledged, the forests, gardens, and hills become dry. Troops of elephants, bringing their young, wander near the city searching for drinkable water. The king's rich concubines, their arms circled with gold, spend lazy days in his embrace, and as reward receive carriages, palanquins, jewel-studded beds, yellow yak's-tail fans, golden betel-boxes, and sharp steel swords. They spend hours of pleasure at the king's side, drinking wine from cups of pure gold brought by slaves. In their drunkenness they beat their bodies at random in an attempt to drive away the flies busy around their flower wreaths. When they laugh, their white teeth seem rows of pearls shining in the jewel case of their red lips. They hum gay songs that forlorn hearts never sing, but when they try to sing, the eight modes from their throats sound coarse, and the listeners laugh. Then the corners of their eyes, long as oars, redden with anger till they seem purple lotus flowers, and pearls of sweat gather on their foreheads, each adorned with a solitary red mark, while they bend the murderous bows of their brows. The sons of noble families look enviously at them, for they are meant for the pleasure of only the lord of the universe.

Kôvalan wandered along the main street, bordered by luxurious villas, which ruling kings secretly visit, and which are the homes of courtesans exempt from the tiles duty, and dancers who are masters in the art of street performance *(vêttiyal)* as well as palace shows *(poduviyal)*. They knew the four kinds of music, the seven scales, the songs, the rhythms, the art of oboe playing, and that of accompaniment on leather drums. A singing mistress *(tôriamadandai)* sang a melody *(vâram)*, while other women spun thread or wove beautiful wreaths. In the shops Kôvalan noticed steel saws, tools for carving ivory, incense, pastes, and flower bouquets so rich and colorful that kings might have envied them.

Kôvalan then entered the jewelers' special street that no enemy had ever plundered. There shining diamonds were sold, without flaw or stain or crow's-foot, or any fault an expert could detect. The diamonds had the hues of the four castes: [white, red, yellow, and black]. Cloudless green emeralds, perfect in form and luster, could be purchased. The rubies called red lotuses *(padmam)*, the sapphires *(nîlam)*, the pearls *(bindu)*, the crystals *(sphatika)*—all seemed of stainless perfection. A cat's-eye *(pushpa-râga)*, mounted on gold, cast glances that were just like a real cat's. Attractive gold sardonyx shone like the sun, onyx seemed made of solid night, the two-colored opals and the five lucky gems that come from the same mines showed all the colors of sunset. There were also heaps of white and pink pearls, and some of more subtle orient. None showed the defects that wind, sand, rocks, or sea water may cause. There were also branches of red coral, not twisted or with stones imbedded in them.

In the broad street of the goldsmiths tiny flags marked the kind of gold sold in each shop: natural gold, green gold resembling parrots' wings, and fine gold from Jâmbûnada. In the street of the cloth merchants Kôvalan made his way through piles of bales, each containing a hundred lengths, woven of cotton, hair, or silk. There was a street for grain merchants, busy with their balances, measures, and bushels. Bags of grain and pepper were to be found there in all seasons. Kôvalan also visited the four residential quarters of the four castes. He saw crossings of three or of four roads, bazaars, squares, avenues lined with trees, and many smaller streets and lanes. Beyond the ramparts, he noticed bowers covered with green creepers that never let the sun's burning rays penetrate. He felt pleased to have seen this splendid and glorious city that a noble Pândya king protects against all ills.

✗✗ CANTO FIFTEEN ✗✗

The Refuge

Adaikkalakkâdai

Kôvalan wandered through the vast old city of Madurai, famed for the equity of its kings, the blessings of peace it enjoys under their stainless parasol, and the daring conquests of the Kauriyar's spear. Guided by Providence, the king, who moves the unwieldy wheel of justice with circumspection, has never been betrayed by his faithful subjects.

Kôvalan returned to the grove beyond the walls, where the monks live and teach Dharma, the Law of Perfection. While he was depicting to Kavundi the splendor of the town and the prowess of the Pândya monarch, a good Brahmin named Mâdalan, learned in the four *Vedas*, came to their camp in the shady garden enclosed by a narrow ditch. He was from the village of Talaicchengânam, and wanted to rest before returning home after ritually bathing at the Cape and walking around the sage's mountain.

Kôvalan bowed, and the Brahmin, adroit in dialectics, told him:

"After Mâdhavi, more tender than a mango shoot, had obtained, in reward for her dance, the precious gift of your substance, she became pregnant and gave birth to a delicate girl. You showed some interest in the babble of old dancers who were pondering about a good name for the child. You told them: 'One of my ancestors was on a ship that sank during the night in the middle of the ocean. He had numerous noble deeds to his credit and found in them the strength to remain afloat several days. The goddess of the Sea then appeared to him and said, "I come at the bidding of Indra, king of the gods. People call me Precious-Girdle *(Mani-mêkalai)*. Do not fear! The merits of your good actions have not been lost: they shall help you to cross this vast ocean of pain." And she saved him, leading him to the shore. This goddess has long been the divinity who protects my clan. I want her name to be given to the infant.' Then more than a thou-

99

sand courtesans, their girdles studded with rare gems, came and blessed the child, naming her Precious-Girdle.

"You were near the happy Mâdhavi, giving gold coins to everyone with your beautiful hands. A Brahmin, bent under the weight of age, who had attained the highest peaks of wisdom and virtue, came leaning on a staff to receive your presents. As he was approaching, an angry elephant, throwing off his mahout, ran furiously about. Warning drums were sounded. The elephant knocked down the elderly Brahmin. Then, generous hero, you jumped up with a gasp, and saved the noble man. Disentangling yourself from the beast's trunk and seizing its tusks, you jumped up on its neck and mastered its fury. You looked like an angel of wisdom standing on a mountain of sin.

"On another occasion, a Brahmin left for the north, abandoning his wife, who had unintentionally killed a little mongoose. When she wanted to follow him, the Brahmin scolded her: 'All food that your hands can prepare is now, for me, forbidden food. Take this palm leaf, on which is written a Sanskrit verse. You may show it to men of sound virtue.' The Brahmin's wife wandered through the bazaars where the rich merchants had their homes. There she cried, 'He who shall buy away my sin shall acquire great merit.' You sent for her, and you inquired, 'Why are you in distress, and what is written on this leaf?' The poor woman explained her plight, and said, 'Please buy this leaf on which a verse has been inscribed, for, when you purchase it, my fault shall be redeemed!' You replied to her, 'Be at peace, for I shall relieve you of your grief.' So that her fault might be absolved, you performed the charities prescribed by tradition, and her plight was ended. You are strong, and so rich that your treasure seems inexhaustible. You recalled the husband from his forest retreat and endowed them both generously with a small part of your wealth.

"Once a virtuous woman had been wrongly accused. A false witness, who had told lies to her husband, was captured in a net by a *bhûtam*, a fearful genie who devoured all villains of his sort. Though the fault was grave, moved by the great sorrow of the man's old mother, you threw yourself into the net and said to the honest and well-meaning genie, 'Give back this man's life and take mine instead.' He refused, arguing, 'There is no rule that may permit me to exchange a good man's life for that of a scoundrel. Should I obey you, I might lose the happiness that will be mine in future lives. So give up this scheme.' When the genie, in your presence, had eaten up the culprit, you, O master of great wealth, accompanied the heartbroken woman home, and for many years, like a son, you kept her from hunger.

"I know of countless noble deeds you performed in this life. Yet for some errors committed in a past existence, wise Kôvalan, you shall fall into fearful calamities, bringing misfortune to your precious and innocent consort, beautiful as Lakshmî, the goddess of Fortune."

Kôvalan answered him:

"Half asleep in the deepest night, I had a fearful dream: In this town, over which a righteous king rules, through the fault of a scoundrel this girl with the five fragrant plaits underwent a fearful agony; while I, stripped of my garments by some stranger, was riding a huge buffalo with black horns. But later, with my gentle wife whose hair curls so gracefully, I reached a divine land where those freed from terrestrial bonds may dwell. I also saw Mâdhavi giving her child, Precious-Girdle, to a

Buddhist nun, while the god of Love in despair could find no target but the naked earth at which to shoot his flowery arrows."

The good Brahmin and Kavundi then quickly said: "This shelter outside the ramparts is meant for the rest of saintly monks. Go to the town. Look for a proper place to stay. Some merchant, when he hears your name, will be glad to offer you his hospitality. Go, before darkness comes, and enter this city of many rich mansions."

Mâdari, an old woman who herded cows, was just coming home after bringing an offering of milk, as was her daily practice, to a *yakshinî*, a flower-eyed young fairy who dwelt in a small shrine outside the ramparts, near a field where the monks assemble for their meditation. She bowed to Kavundi. In her heart the saint felt: the life of these cowherds, who attend to dumb animals and offer to the gods the produce of their herd, is pure of all evil. This old woman is still as innocent as a child. She is virtuous and kind. There can be no danger in leaving Kannaki in her care.

So she said to Mâdari:

"When the merchants of this city discover who is the father-in-law of this girl, they will invite her and her husband into their well-guarded homes, considering it a privilege. Until we can bring her to these wealthy mansions, keep Kannaki under your protection. Give her a good cool bath and put black collyrium on her long, reddened eyes. Rearrange her hair with fresh flowers. Dress her in a well-washed garment, as is proper for people of her rank. Be her servant, for she is of high birth; but be also her mother and guardian. Take care of her. Our mother Earth has shown no pity for her tender feet during our long journey. Thirst made her faint in the hot sun, yet, forgetting her pain, she thought only of her husband. There was never a goddess more radiant than this woman, made for heaven, who keeps the vow of faithfulness by which a wife is bound to her husband. Have you not heard the saying: 'Where a woman's virtue is safe and unsullied, the blessings of rain never fail, prosperity never declines, victory is ever a slave to the monarch!'

"Listen! However small the sum entrusted to your care by a saint, it multiplies a hundredfold. A wandering yogi, a *charanar*, once taught Dharma, the Law, in a city overlooking the Kaveri. He sat on a polished rock throne, erected by pious *shâvakas*, under the shade of an *ashoka* in blossom. Standing before the sage while he preached, there was a god, radiant as the sun, handsome and strong, adorned with flowers, gems, and gold finery. He shone like the rainbow, and several other gods were seen to worship him. Yet one of his hands was black and like a monkey's. The pious *shâvakas*, who came to bow before the sage, often wondered about the apparition of this remarkable god. One day the sage told them:

"'Long ago there lived a merchant named Etti Shâyalan. Many were the people who came to converse with him on fast days. Once the lady of the house had received with great honors a very saintly monk. At the same moment a monkey had entered and thrown himself at the feet of the holy man. Hungry, he ate remnants of food and some water left by the monk, and then sat motionless in deep contemplation. The wise yogi had attained perfect peace. He rejoiced in his heart and said to the woman, "From now on, this monkey shall be your son." The good lady obeyed the order of the saint, and, when the affectionate monkey died, she distributed to the monks that part of the patrimony that is set aside for a son, praying that all the monkey's sins be remitted. This monkey was reborn as the most worthy son of Uttara-gautta, the king of Benares, in the central country. Famous for his beauty, his wealth, and his wisdom, he died at thirty-two. Later he obtained the status of prince among the gods, and he has returned to life with his black monkey hand so that virtuous Jains may know the secret of his achievements. He is here to tell us, "My fortune and felicity are fruits of the kindness of her who gave me protection and love. Previously I was just a monkey; my metamorphosis is the wonderful gift of Shâyalan's good wife." All the people who listened to the monk realized that his words were inspired. The ascetics of the country, the virtuous Jains with their wives, the good Etti and his consort—all were granted immortal life.'

"Now that you have heard all these tales, take this woman, whose hair is loaded with flowers, along with you. Waste no time."

At Kavundi's words, Mâdari was filled with joy. She paid her respects to the saint, and at sunset took her leave. Beautiful Kannaki, with her tender breasts, shoulders like bending reeds, and gleaming teeth, followed the good cowherd woman. As they went she heard cows mooing to their calves. Soon they met the shepherds, with lambs on their shoulders, carrying axes and long staves from which hung jars full of pure milk. All the cowherd girls wore showy bracelets.

Mâdari, with her protégée, passed the city gate where every day a new pennant was raised to announce a victory. The ramparts were topped with junglelike overgrowth as additional protection. There was also a moat, above which they could see arbalests for shooting arrows great distances. There was a catching device with its black pincers, catapults for throwing stones, huge cauldrons to hold boiling water or molten lead, hooks, chains, and traps resembling *ândalai* birds [with a man's head and a beak that breaks skulls]. There were also other weapons of many kinds: iron arms, sharp spears, heaps of arrows and nails, rams, sharp needles to pierce eyes, machines resembling kingfishers used to put out eyes, wooden balls covered with sharp nails, machines to strike blows, heavy weights, huge beams, maces, and projectiles. Finally Mâdari led Kannaki into her cottage.

✣✣ CANTO SIXTEEN ✣✣

The Site of Agony

Kolaikkalakkâdai

Mâdari the cowherdess had joyfully taken charge of the frail Kannaki. In the sheltered cottage to which she led her, cowgirls lived who wore shining bracelets. The cottage was dark red. In front was an open courtyard. Thorny hedges kept it private from other huts inhabited by the cowherds who sold buttermilk.

Mâdari prepared a cool bath for the stranger and paid her compliments:

"You have come here, adorned only by your beauty, to render ridiculous the cosmetics and costly jewelry of the city women. My daughter Aiyai will be at your service, and I shall protect you like a precious object. O girl with fragrant hair entrusted to my care, the virtuous saint has relieved you of the weariness of your journey, and led you to a safe retreat. Your man need not worry."

Turning toward the girls, she said: "Her master observes all the rules of the pious Jains, who do not eat after sunset. Bring at once our best saucepans so that Kannaki may help Aiyai to prepare a good meal."

The cowgirls brought new utensils, as is done for wealthy people, and some ripe fruit from the never-flowering breadfruit tree. There were also white-striped cucumbers, green pomegranates and mangoes, sweet bananas, good rice, and fresh cow's milk. The girls said:

"Lady with the round bracelets, accept these modest gifts."

Kannaki sliced various vegetables with a short knife: her tender fingers grew red, her face was perspiring, tears came to her lovely eyes. She had to turn her face away from the oven. Over a straw fire lit by Aiyai, Kannaki began to prepare her husband's evening meal.

Kôvalan seated himself on a small expertly woven palm-leaf mat. Then Kannaki, with her flower-hands, poured water from a jug to wash her master's feet. As if attempting to awaken our mother Earth from a swoon, she sprinkled water on the ground and lustrated the beaten soil with her palms. Then she placed before her husband a tender plantain leaf and said:

"Here is your food, my lord! May you be pleased to eat."

Having performed with care the rites prescribed for the sons of merchants, they ate their dinner together. Aiyai and her mother looked at them with delight. They exclaimed:

"The noble lord, eating this simple food, must be Krishna himself, whose complexion is like newly open pepper flowers. Krishna too was fed in a cowherd's village, by Yashodâ. Is not this lady of the many bracelets the beacon of our caste, who once rescued the god who is the color of blue sapphire near the Jumna River? We cannot open our eyes wide enough to enjoy this rare sight!"

To tall Kôvalan, pleased with his dinner, Kannaki of the gleaming black plaits then offered betel leaves and chopped betel nuts. He embraced her and said:

"My parents would never believe that such tender feet could have trodden paths littered with pebbles and hard stones. Would they not pity you if they knew that we had together crossed such vast and cruel country? It all seems to me like a dream, like a game played by fate. My mind is dull: I fail to understand. Is there any hope left for a man who wasted his youth in the pernicious company of debauched friends, laughing at vulgar deeds and scandals, seeking mischief, and neglectful of the warning words of his wise elders? I neglected all my duties toward my good parents. I was a source of shame to you, so young in years yet so rich in wisdom. I did not see the extent of my faults. I asked you not to leave our city, yet you came with me on this long journey. What sufferings have you not already borne for my sake!"

Kannaki answered:

"In my husband's absence, I could not distribute presents to good men, honor Brahmins, welcome saintly monks, or receive friends, as is done in all noble homes. After your desertion I tried to hide my tears from your respected mother and your renowned and proud father, whom the king holds in high esteem. Yet they understood my sorrow, showed me their affection, and spoke to me kindly. In spite of my efforts to smile, the feebleness of my body betrayed to them the anguish of my heart. You may have gone astray from the path of virtue, but I wished to do my duty, and so I followed you."

Kôvalan said:

"You left your old parents, your friends, your attendants, your nurse, and all your retinue, and kept at your service only your modesty, your faith, your virtue, and your loyalty. You came with me and relieved me of remorse. Precious as a golden liana, girl with the fragrant plaits! You are the incarnation of faithfulness, the beacon of the world, the tender bud of chastity, the store of all virtues. I must now go to the town, taking with me one of the gold circlets that grace your charming ankles. Having exchanged it for money, I shall soon return. Till then do not let your courage fail."

After kissing the long black hair he loved, heart-broken to leave her all alone, and holding back the tears that filled his eyes, he walked heavily away. As a stranger to those parts, he could not know that the humped bull that stood before him as he passed the meeting place of the cowherds was a fearful omen.

Passing through the street of the courtesans, he reached the bazaar. There he saw a goldsmith in court dress, who was walking along, tweezers in hand, followed by a hundred jewelers all famous for their craftsmanship. Kôvalan thought this must be the goldsmith of the Pândya monarch. So he approached him and inquired:

"Could you estimate the value of an ankle bracelet worthy of the consort of the great king who protects us?"

The goldsmith had the face of Death's dread messenger. He answered with obsequious politeness:

"I am a novice in this great art: I know only how to make diadems and a few royal ornaments." Kôvalan opened the packet containing the precious anklet. The perfidious goldsmith examined the fine workmanship of the chiseling in pure gold and the rare rubies and diamonds. After a pause he said: "This circlet can be purchased only by the great queen herself. I am going to the palace, and shall speak to the victorious king. You may wait with the anklet near my humble home till I return."

Kôvalan sat down in a small shrine that stood near the villain's cottage. When he saw him waiting in the narrow temple, the hardhearted thief thought: Before anyone discovers that it was I who stole the [queen's] anklet, I shall accuse this foreigner before the king. He then walked on.

The great queen, resentful of the king's interest in Madurai's pretty dancers, who sing songs of all sorts and show in their movements their understanding of music, was disguising her jealousy under the mask of a friendly quarrel. Pretending a sudden headache, she left the royal presence. Later, when ministers and counselors had gone, the king entered the inner apartment where the great queen lay surrounded by maids with long alluring eyes.

The goldsmith met the king near the innermost door, where guards had been posted. He bowed low, praising the monarch in a hundred ways. Then he said:

"The man who stole an anklet from this palace has been found. He apparently did not use heavy tools or crowbars, but just the power of magic words, with which he put to sleep the soldiers who were guarding the doors. He then quietly took away the handsomest ankle bracelet in the palace. He is now hiding near my humble house, fearing the guards that patrol the city."

Now it befell that this was the moment when the actions of Kôvalan's past lives had become ripe like a mature crop in the fields. The king, who wears the garland of margosa leaves, did not call for any inquiry. He simply summoned some town guards and ordered:

"Should you find, in the hands of a most clever thief, an ankle ornament resembling a wreath of flowers, which belongs to my consort, put the man to death and bring me the bracelet."

When he heard the royal order, the infamous goldsmith, with mirth in his heart, thought: I've brought it off! He led the guards to Kôvalan, whom a merciless fate had thrown into his net, and told him:

"On orders from the king, whose army has won all battles, these officers have come with me to look at your piece of jewelry." He pointed out to them the details of the ankle bracelet's design. But they protested:

"The appearance of this good man is surely not that of a thief. We cannot put him to death."

The astute goldsmith smiled contemptuously. He explained to these simple men that the people whose shameful trade is theft have invented eight ways to deceive their innocent victims: these are spells, bewitching, drugs, omens, and magic, as well as place, time, and devices.

"If you let yourselves become intoxicated by the drugs this man dares use, you expose yourselves to the anger of our great king.

"The thief who utters magic spells becomes invisible, like a child of the gods. When he calls for the help of celestial genii, he can carry away his stolen objects unseen. Stupefying his victims with his drugs, he renders them incapable of the slightest movement. Unless omens are good, a real thief abstains from any activity even when he sees before him objects of great value ready to fall into his hands. When he makes use of enchantments, he can despoil the king of the gods himself of the wreath that adorns his chest. If he has chosen in advance the place of his rapine, no one can see him there. When he has set the time, the gods themselves could not stop him from seizing the object he wants. If he uses his implements to steal things of great value, no one can find him out. If you should read in the thieves' sacred book, you would see that their art requires arduous study, and that it has almost no limits.

"It happened once that a clever thief, disguised as an ambassador, had stood a whole day before the door of the palace. At night he changed himself into a young woman, and, entering unnoticed, hid in the shadow cast by a lamp. He seized the rare diamond necklace, bright as the sun, that shone round the neck of the sleeping crown prince. Waking up, the prince felt that his necklace was not on his shoulders. He drew his sword, but the thief was able to grasp it and keep the prince from striking a blow. When he tired of this, the prince tried fighting with his hands, but the thief, expert in his profession, ran away, leaving the prince alone and fighting against a stone pillar studded with precious gems. There is no thief on earth equal to this villain. If one of you has a better one, then he may bring him to me."

A young hangman who had been listening to the criminal goldsmith's words, spear in hand, said:

"In the season of rains, during a dark night when my village was fast asleep, a thief came armed with a ploughshare like those used in the fields. Dressed in black, searching for jewels, he seemed fiercer than a tiger. I drew my sword but he tore it away from me and vanished, never to be found. The deeds of thieves are amazing. If we do not obey the king, we shall surely be in trouble. Brave soldiers, let's do our duty."

Thereupon one of these drunkards hurled his sword at Kôvalan. It pierced his body. Blood gushing from the wound fell upon the Earth, mother of men, and she shuddered with grief. Defeated by his fate, Kôvalan fell; and the virtuous scepter of the Pândyas was bent.

CODA

And since the champion of justice
failed to safeguard Kannaki's beloved spouse,
the upright scepter of the Pândya kings
became forever bent.
All these events had been foreseen,

for actions, be they good or evil,
bear their inexorable fruits.
This is the reason that wise men
make all their actions
accord with the great moral laws.

❉❦ CANTO SEVENTEEN ❉❦

The Dance of the Cowgirls

Âcchiyarkuravai

"Soon we shall hear the morning drums sounded in the palace of the Pândya, whose immaculate parasol, embellished with festoons, is respected by the whole world. No king in India, land of rosewood, covered with deep forests, dares challenge his rule. The Chôla and Chêra kings of Chôlamandala and Kerala, who carved their own emblems, the tiger and the bow, upon the Himalayan rocks, must acknowledge him paramount.

"This morning it will be our turn to prepare the butter."

Thus spoke old Mâdari, calling her daughter Aiyai, who came bringing the rope and the pestle.

INTERLUDE

Uraippâttumadai

Aiyai exclaimed:
"Alas! The milk did not curd in the jar.
The handsome eyes of the bulls

are full of tears. Tragedy is about.
The sweet-smelling butter does not melt in the pan.
The lambs are silent. Disaster is abroad.
The cows, their udders full,
are shivering; the bells fall from their necks.
Catastrophe is in the air."

THE SIGNIFICANCE

Karuppam

Milk that will not curd in the jar, bulls' eyes that become tender and tearful, butter that will not melt in the pan, lamps that burn with an unflickering flame, bells that fall to the ground—these are terrible omens. Mâdari looked at her daughter and said:

"Don't fear! To calm the frightened cattle, we shall perform the dance of love in the presence of Kannaki, precious jewel among the daughters of the earth." This love-dance shows one of the games young Krishna and Balarâma, his elder, had played on the dance-ground of the cowherds with the darling Pinnai, whose eyes looked like the points of lances.

THE ANNOUNCEMENT

Kolu

Mâdari, pointing at one of the girls, announced:

"This charming woman with the flower wreath shall give her heart to him who rides the huge black bull.

"The lovely shoulders of the girl with gold rings are for the fortunate suitor who can master the bull with red marks on its head.

"The girl whose lovely hair is crowned with jasmine shall be the wife of anyone who can ride this strong and petulant young bull.

"The shoulders of this lianalike girl shall be for him who can master the bull with white markings.

"The tender breasts of this sinuous woman shall belong only to the boy who can conquer the bull with golden markings.

"The maiden whose hair is adorned with laburnum flowers will be taken as bride by him who can ride this fierce bull.

"This girl who resembles a flower bud shall belong to the man who can control the bull as white as milk."

DESIGNATIONS

Eduttukkâttu

When the seven maidens had each taken from the herd the bull that she had brought up, Mâdari placed the girls in line and gave each a role to play. Going from west to east, she called them Do, Re, Mi, Fa, Sol, La, and Si: such were the odd names bestowed by the fragrant-haired Mâdari. The girl who was Do played the part of Krishna (Mâyavan). Sol was the valiant Balarâma, high-pitched Si was Pinnai, the divine cowherdess. The others were given their names in order. Pinnai, the Si, stood near Mâyavan; Fa and La joined the white Balarâma; Mi came next to Re, and the honest La stood to the right of Si. All those who came to place a garland of tulsi around Mâyavan's neck had to dance, without one mistake, the dance of love.

"Is Pinnai, her arms loaded with bracelets, so charming that he who crossed the world in three great strides forgets to look at his consort Lakshmî (Fortune), curled up against his chest?"
And Mâdari laughed.

THE DANCE

Kûttulpadutal

They stood in a circle, holding each other's hands with the crab's grip, and all began to dance. First the girl who was Do looked at her neighbor Re, and said:
"Let's sing the mode of the jasmine (*mullai*) for him who uprooted the [demon disguised as a] citrus tree that stood in the middle of the great meadow."
Do first gave out her low note, next Sol her median sound, and then Si her high pitch. Lastly the girl who was La sounded her note, less high-pitched than that of her neighbor Si.

SONGS

Friends! Mâyavan swung a calf like a slung stone,
and knocked down all the orchard's fruit.
If he came down to see our herd
then we could hear the lovely sound
of his most wondrous flute.

Friends! Mâyavan churned the ocean,
using a snake for rope.
If he came down to tend our herd,
then we could enjoy the sound
of his long bamboo flute.

Friends! Mâyavan tore up the wild citrus tree
that stood in our vast pasture land.
Should he appear amidst our herd,
then we should have a chance to hear
his sweet shepherd's flute.

Let's sing now the bewitching loveliness
of Pinnai, who is dancing near the river
with the boy she loves so tenderly.

How can we describe his magic
when he hid the garments of the girls
whose waists appeared so fragile
that, bending, they might have broken?

How can we describe the face
of the lovely girl distressed by the remorse
of him who stole her dress?

How can we describe the loveliness
of her who stole the heart of him
who loved her but fooled her like the other women
while they were playing in the stream?

How can our words express the charm
of him who took the favors and the rings
of her who stole his heart?

How can we picture the sweet face
she hid behind her lovely hands
when he had stolen her garments and her jewels?

And how can we describe the grace
of his repentance when he saw
with what distress
she hid the fairness of her face
within the darkness of her hands?

Onran pakuti

Now to the left of Pinnai, whose dark hair
is bright with flower blossoms, stands
the god whose color is the sea's, and hides
the sun behind the discus that he holds
in his divine hand of lotus.
And to the right of Pinnai stands
—his body whiter than the Moon—
the pale elder brother.

Among the famed musicians
who accompanied young Pinnai's dance
is Nârada, singer of the *Vedas*,
he who marked the rhythm
on the harp's longest string.
Pinnai, with her head bent, stands to right
of Mâyavan, dark as the peacock's neck,
while to her left the elder brother
stands, whiter than a lotus stem.
And he who plucks the harp's first string
and beats the time for her
is the well-known precentor, Nârada.

IN HONOR OF THE DANCERS

Âdunarppukaldal

The dance of love made famous by Yashodâ
was splendidly performed around the meeting ground
by Mâyavan and by his elder brother,
with Pinnai wearing striped armlets.
The flower garlands in disorder fell
out of the cowgirls' dark and curly hair,

while they were marking time by clapping
hands loaded with gold bangles. "Listen,
my friends!" cried Mâdari. "Let's all sing
the masks' song honoring the god
who rides upon the bird, Garuda.
Hail to him! Hail to him! Hail to him!"

BLESSINGS OF THE HILL DANCERS

Ulvarivâlttu

Upon the chest of the Pândya king is seen
a fretwork, drawn with white sandal paste
brought from Mount Podiyil.
He also wears a string of pearls
and a precious necklace, gift of heaven's king.
They say that he who wears the necklace
of heaven's king is the famed hero who
once tended herds at the *gokula,*
the cow-school near Dvârakâ,
and who dared uproot the citrus tree.

Valavan, the king who rules
Puhâr, that mighty city, had
his emblem, a swift tiger, carved
upon the Himalaya's golden peak,
and thus became the master of the world.
They say that the great Valavan,
king of Puhâr, that mighty city, has
a golden discus for his weapon.

The Chêra, king of kings, who rules
the prosperous Vanji, crossed

over the seas, and put to death
the never-aging *kadamba* tree.
They say too that the king of kings
who rules the prosperous Vanji, is
Vishnu himself, who shakes
his mountainlike shoulders
while he churns the sea.

HYMN OF GLORY

Munnilaipparaval

God, blue as the ocean!
When you churned the womb of the sea,
the churn's pestle was the polar mountain,
the rope the coiled snake of the ages.

God! A lotus springs forth from your navel,
your hands, that once churned the ocean,
were tied by Yashodâ with a churning rope.
Is that an example of your magic?
Your designs are ever mysterious.

God! The hosts of gods and angels
worship you and sing your glory,
you who, in three strides of your lotus feet,
encompassed all the worlds, and banished night.

Man-lion, destroyer of all enemies,
the blessed feet that strode across the worlds
became the heralds of the five Pândavas.
Is this an example of your magic?
Your designs are ever mysterious.

INDIRECT PRAISE

Patarkkaipparaval

Vain are the ears that are not filled
with the great doings of the hero
who, in three strides, encompassed the three worlds
become too narrow for his fame; and who,
together with his younger brother,
went through fearful jungles.
His lotus feet were bruised.
In battle he destroyed the fortress,
and razed the walls of ancient Lankâ.

Vain are the ears that are not filled
with the exploits of the great god.
Vain are the eyes that do not see the god,
the dark god, the mysterious god.
For from his lotus navel the three worlds bloom.
His eyes are red. Red are his feet,
red his hands, and red his lips.
Vain are the eyes that do not see
the dark beauty of the great lord.

Vain is the tongue that does not sing the praise
of him who countered Kamsa's dark intrigues.
Accompanied by singing of the *Vedas*,
he went to meet the hundred Kauravas
as messenger from the five brothers.
Vain is the tongue that does not sing the praise
of him, Nârâyana, the shelter of mankind.
May the god we honor through his love-dance here
show mercy on us now,
for fear has spread upon our herds.

The Pândya king, who wears rich ornaments
across his broad shoulders,
defeated Indra, whose mighty arm

was the dread thunderbolt.
May the sound of the drum of his glory
strike terror in the hearts of all his enemies,
and may he every day announce new victories.

CANTO EIGHTEEN ✹ ★

The Wreath of Agony

Tumbamâlai

Other hardy and shapely cowgirls had been bathing in
the deep waters of the Vaigai. On their return they
worshiped Vishnu, offering him flowers, incense, sandalwood, and fragrant wreaths. Toward the end of the
love-dance, a girl who had heard some rumors in the city
returned in haste. She stopped, silent and motionless, at
some distance from Kannaki, who asked:

"Will you not speak to me, my friend? Tell me. My
husband has not yet returned, and my heart feels oppressed. My breath is as hot as that from a blacksmith's
bellows. Have you not brought some news from the city?
Long may you live, my friend.

"Though the sun is still high, I am trembling. Why
has my beloved not come back? My heart is becoming
heavy with fear. Since you see that I am worried by his
absence, please distract me with some gossip from town.
May the gods bless you, friend.

"Shall I beg your help? My lord has not yet returned.
I fear he may be in danger. My mind is bewildered; I
feel anxious. Are you hiding something from me? Pray
speak to me, my friend. Tell me what people who live in
your city, strangers to me, have said."

At last the cowgirl spoke:

"They abused him. They said he was a thief, come secretly to steal a wonderful ankle bracelet from the royal palace. They accused him, calling him a robber, mysterious in his behavior. And the royal soldiers, those who wear noisy anklets, put him to death."

On hearing this, Kannaki leaped up in her anger, then collapsed to the ground. It seemed as if the moon had risen in the sky; then fallen, shrouded with clouds. She wept, and her eyes became still redder. She clamored, "Where are you, beloved husband?" and fell in a swoon. When she came back to her senses, she lamented:

"And must I die of sorrow, like the wretched women who take fearful oaths upon the pyres of their beloved husbands? For I have lost the man who dearly loved me, by the fault of a king his own subjects must despise.

"Must I die of despair, like the lonely women who carry their grief from pilgrimage to pilgrimage, and bathe in holy rivers, after the death of husbands who wore fragrant flower-garlands on their broad chests?

"Must I die, an embodiment of meaningless virtue, through the fatal error of a ruler who bears the scepter of injustice? Must I languish in loneliness, like the forlorn women who, after their tender husbands have vanished in the funeral pyre's smoke, remain, half alive, in abject widowhood?

"Must I, with broken heart, suffer an endless agony, because in tragic error the scepter of a Pândya king has gone astray from the path of right?

"Look at me! Hearken to my words, you honest cowgirls here assembled! It was with just foreboding that you danced the dance of love. Now hearken to my words! Listen to me, cowherds' daughters!

"Sun god, whose rays are flames! You, the eternal witness of all the deeds committed on the sea-encircled earth, speak! Could my husband be called a thief?"

A voice was heard, coming from the sky:

"He was never a thief! Woman of the carplike eyes, this city shall be purified by fire!"

✺ CANTO NINETEEN ✺

The Murmurs of the City

Urshûlvari

The Sun had given its verdict. The woman with the bright armlets stood up. Holding in her hand her remaining ankle bracelet, mate to the one she had given to Kôvalan, Kannaki went to the city, and walked through it, crying:

"Virtuous women who live in this city ruled by a nefarious monarch, listen to me! Today I underwent unspeakable agony. What must nowise happen has happened. Never shall I accept this iniquitous injustice. Was my husband a thief? No, he was killed to avoid paying him the price of my ankle bracelet. Can there be a more flagrant denial of justice? Should I ever see the body of the man who dearly loved me, I shall not hear from him the words I need to hear, saying he is not at fault. Is that justice? He can no longer protect me, so why don't you come and accuse me too of some invented crime? Do you hear me?"

The people of the rich city of Madurai were dismayed at the sight of this distracted woman. In their stupefaction, they exclaimed:

"The just and virtuous scepter of our king has been forever bent. A crime that nothing can undo has been committed against this innocent woman. What shall this lead us to? Tarnished is the honor of Tennavan, the king of kings, who inherited an infallible spear and a stainless white parasol. What are we to think? The parasol of our victorious king was protecting the land, keeping us cool under its shade; and now the fierce rays of the sun may devour us. What are we to expect?

"A new and mighty goddess has appeared to us. In her hand she carries an ankle bracelet made of gold. Is this a portent from heaven? From the desperate woman's eyes, red and running with black collyrium, tears are flowing. She seems possessed by a genie. What must we think?"

Thus bewildered, the people of Madurai gathered around her, showing their good will and attempting to console her. Everywhere indignant words could be heard. In the midst of this disorder, someone showed Kannaki the body of her dear husband. The lianalike woman saw him; he could not see her.

The Sun was unable to bear this sight. Suddenly it extinguished its rays, hiding behind the hills. The veil of night covered the earth. In the evening dusk Kannaki, resembling a frail reed in bloom, lamented, and the whole city resounded with her cries. That very morning, between two kisses, she had received from her husband a flower wreath he was wearing, and with it she had adorned her tresses. Now on the evening of the same day she looked down at him lying in a pool of blood that had flowed from his open wound. He could not even see her grief. She cried out in anger and despair:

"O witness of my grief, you cannot console me. Is it right that your body, fairer than pure gold, lie unwashed here in the dust? Will people not say that it was my ill luck that led a just king to a mistake that was the fruit of his ignorance? Is it just that in the red glow of the twilight your handsome chest, framed with a flower wreath, lies thrown down on the bare earth, while I remain alone, helpless and abandoned to despair? Shall people not be led to say that it was my own predestination that compelled the innocent Pândya to such an injustice when the whole world could easily see that he had committed an error?

"Is there no woman here? Is there no real woman, or only the sort of woman who would allow such an injustice to be done to her lawful husband? Are there such women here?

"Is there no man in this land? Is there no honest man, or only the sort of man who nourishes and protects only the sons of his own blood?

"Is there no god? Is there no god in this country? Can there be a god in a land where the sword of the king is used for the murder of innocent strangers? Is there no god, no god?"

Thus lamenting, Kannaki clasped her husband's chest that Fortune had so dearly cherished. Suddenly Kôvalan arose and exclaimed, "Your moonlike face appears tarnished." With affectionate hands he wiped away the tears that burned her eyes. The lovely woman fell to the ground, weeping and moaning. With bracelet-laden hands she grasped the feet of her beloved husband. But he departed, rising into the air. Surrounded by hosts of angels, he shed his mortal frame and disappeared. His voice could still be heard, fading away:

"Beloved! Stay there, stay! Remain peacefully in life!"

She thought: Is this an illusion of my demented mind? What else could all this be? Is some spirit eager to deceive me? Where can I discover the truth? I shall not search for my husband before he is avenged. I shall meet this inhuman king and ask for his justice against himself.

She stood up, and then she remembered her vision. Tears fell from her long carp-shaped eyes. She stiffened, and recalled her anger. Wiping away her burning tears, she ran to the majestic gate of the royal palace.

CANTO TWENTY

The Call for Justice

Valakkuraikâdai

The Pândya queen spoke:

"Alas! I saw, in a dream, a scepter bent, a fallen parasol. The bell at the gate moved of itself and rang loudly. Alas! I also saw . . . I saw the eight directions of space wavering, the night devouring the sun. Alas! I also saw . . . I saw the rainbow shining in the night, a glittering star falling by day. Alas!"

THE OMENS

"The scepter of justice and the white parasol fallen to the hard ground, the bell ringing alone at the gate of a victorious king's palace, my heart trembling with fear, the rainbow in the night, the star falling by day, the directions of space vacillating—all these are portents of a fearful danger at hand. I must inform the king."

Adorned with resplendent jewels, she went to the king's apartments, followed by maids who carried her mirror and her various trifles. With her went her hunchbacks, dwarfs, deaf-mutes, and buffoons, carrying silks, betel, cosmetics, pastes, garlands, feather-fans, and incense. The ladies in waiting, with flowers in their hair, sang her praise:

"May the consort of the Pândya, who protects the vast universe, live many happy days."

Thus the great queen, followed by her guards and maids singing her praises and bowing before her feet, went to King Tennavan, on whose chest Fortune rests. He was seated on the lion throne. She told him her sinister dream.

At the same moment cries were heard:

"Hoy, doorkeeper! Hoy, watchman! Hoy, palace guards of an irresponsible ruler whose vile heart lightly casts aside the kingly duty of rendering justice! Go! Tell how a woman, a widow, carrying a single ankle bracelet from a pair that once joyfully rang together, waits at the gate. Go! Announce me!"

The watchman bowed before the king and said:

"Long live the ruler of Korkai! Long live Tennavan, lord of the southern mountains, whose fair name calumny and scandal have never touched!

"A woman is waiting at the gate. She is not Korravai, the victorious goddess who carries in her hand a glorious spear and stands upon the neck of a defeated buffalo losing its blood through its fresh wounds. She is not Anangu, youngest of the seven virgins, for whom Shiva once danced; and she is not Kâlî, who dwells in the darkest forests inhabited by ghosts and imps. Neither is she the goddess who pierced the chest of the mighty Dâruka.

She seems filled with a mad fury, suffused with rage. She has lost someone dear to her, and stands at the gate clasping an ankle bracelet of gold in her hands."

The king said:

"Let her come in. Bring her to me." The gatekeeper let the woman enter, and brought her to the king. When she drew near the monarch, he said: "Woman, your face is soiled from weeping. Who are you, young woman? What brings you before us?"

Kannaki answered sharply:

"Inconsiderate king! I have much to say. I was born in Puhâr, that well-known capital, the names of whose kings remain unsullied. One of them, Shibi, in ancient times sacrificed his own life to save a dove, in the presence of all the gods. Another, Manunîtikanda, when a cow with weeping eyes rang the palace bell in search of justice for her calf, crushed under a chariot wheel, sacrificed his own son, guilty of the act, under the same wheel. There in Puhâr a man named Kôvalan was born. He was the son of a wealthy merchant, Mâshâttuvan. His family is known, and his name untarnished. Led by fate, O king, he entered your city, with ringing anklets, expecting to earn a living. When he tried to sell my ankle bracelet, he was murdered. I am his wife. My name is Kannaki."

The king answered:

"Divine woman, there is no injustice in putting a robber to death. Do you not know that that is the duty of a king?"

The beautiful girl said:

"King of Korkai, you went astray from the path of duty. Remember that my ankle bracelet was filled with precious stones."

"Woman," the king answered, "what you have said is pertinent. For ours was filled, not with gems, but with pearls. Let it be brought." The ankle bracelet was brought and placed before the king. Kannaki seized it and broke it open. A gem sprang up into the king's face. When he saw the stone, he faltered. He felt his parasol fallen, his scepter bent. He said: "Is it right for a king to act upon the word of a miserable goldsmith? I am the thief. For the first time I have failed in my duty as protector of the southern kingdom. No way is left open to me save to give up my life." And having spoken, the king swooned. The great queen fell near him. Trembling, she lamented:

"Never can a woman survive her husband's death." And, placing the feet of her lord on her head, the unfortunate queen fainted away.

Kannaki said:

"Today we have seen evidence of the sage's warning: *The Divine Law appears in the form of death before the man who fails in his duty.* Consort of a victorious king who committed a deed both cruel and unjust! I too am guilty of great sins. Be witness to the cruel deed I perform."

CODA

The poet speaks:

With terror I saw Kannaki, tears streaming from her blood-red eyes, holding in her hand her remaining ankle bracelet, her body lifeless, her undone hair resembling a dark forest.

I saw the sovereign of Kudal become a corpse. I must be guilty of great crimes to be witness to such fearful events.

The lord of the Vaigai saw Kannaki's body, soiled with dust, her black disheveled hair, her tears, and the solitary ankle bracelet in her fair hand. Overwhelmed with sorrow, he listened to the words Kannaki had said in her rage. He could not bear to remain alive, and fell dead.

✣✣ CANTO TWENTY-ONE ✣✣

The Malediction

Vanjinamâlai

Kannaki then spoke to the dying Pândya queen:
"Wife of a great monarch! I too am a victim of fate. I have never wished to cause pain. But it is said that he who has wronged another in the morning must, before darkness falls, repay his debt.

"A woman with abundant hair one day asked and obtained that at midday her kitchen and the oven's fire should take human form to testify to her purity.

"Once, as a joke, her friends told a virtuous and naïve widow, whose pubis showed some stripes, that her husband was a sand effigy modeled on the bank of the Kâverî. The faithful woman stayed near the image. The rising tide, which had surrounded her, stayed aloof, not daring to approach.

"A daughter of the famous king, Karikâla, once jumped into the sea that had carried away her husband Vanjikkôn, calling to him, 'Lord with shoulders like mountains!' The god of the Sea himself brought back her husband to her. Clasping him like a liana, she led him to their home.

"Another good woman changed herself into stone and remained in a garden near the shore gazing at the approaching ships. She recovered her human shape only on the day when her husband returned home.

"When the son of a co-wife fell into a well, a woman threw in her own son and succeeded in saving both.

"Because a stranger had glanced at her with lustful eyes, a chaste woman changed her moonlike face into that of a monkey. Only when her husband returned did this flowerlike woman, who treasured her body more than a jewel, take back her human face.

"There was also a girl, fair and lovely as a statue of gold. She heard her mother say to her father, 'Women's settlements unsettle all things. Once, as a joke, I told my maid, "When I have a daughter, and when you, maid with pretty bangles, have a son, my daughter shall be your son's bride." The maid kept this in her memory, and today she asked me for the girl. I am at my wits' end, not knowing what to say. How unfortunate I am!' When she overheard this, the girl like a golden statue put on a silk dress, tied her hair, and came to the maid's son. She knelt before him and placed his foot upon her head.

"It was in Puhâr, the city from which I come, that they all lived, these noble women with fragrant braids. If these stories are true, and if I am faithful, I cannot allow your city to survive. I must destroy it, together with its king. You shall soon see the meaning of my words."

Kannaki then left the king's palace, shouting:

"Men and women of Madurai, city of the four temples! And you, gods of heaven! Listen to me! I curse this town whose ruler put to death the man I dearly loved. The blame is not mine."

Suddenly, with her own hands, she twisted and tore her left breast from her body. Then she walked three times round the city, repeating her curse at each gate. In her despair she threw away her lovely breast, which fell in the dirt of the street. Then before her there appeared the god of Fire in the shape of a priest. His body was all blue and encircled with tongues of flames. His hair was as red as the evening sky, his milk-white teeth shone brightly. He said:

"Faithful woman! I have orders to destroy this city on the very day you suffered such great wrong. Is there someone that should be spared?"

Kannaki bade him:

"Spare Brahmins, good men, cows, truthful women, cripples, old men, children. Destroy evildoers."

And the city of Madurai, capital of the Pândyas, whose chariots are invincible, was immediately hidden in flames and smoke.

CODA

When the glorious Pândya, his dancers and his palace,
his soldiers holding shining bows, even
his elephants, were all burnt down to ashes,
destroyed by the flames of virtue,
the wretched town's immortals went away,
for they are blameless.

✠✠ CANTO TWENTY-TWO ✠✠

The Conflagration

Alarpatukâdai

The swift messenger of the gods exhaled his fiery breath over the city—which its guardian genii were deserting, slamming the gates. Tennavan, the princely knight, to convince his mother, the Earth, that his reign had been one of honor, had, together with his queen of stainless repute, given up his life. He thus repaid the debt of shame that had bent his scepter and smeared his throne with blood.

Not understanding that the king and queen were dead on the steps of the throne, the palace priests and astrologers, the judges and treasurer, the learned ministers, together with the maids of honor and the servants, waited motionless like the painted figures of a fresco. Suddenly elephants and their drivers, horsemen, charioteers, and brutal sword-wielding soldiers, terrified by the flames, all ran from the palace and attempted to control the fire. It was then that the four genii who protect the four castes prepared to abandon the town.

The first genie, of the priestly order, had the color of the moon and of pearls. He wore a rich necklace and other ornaments. Around his hair-tuft, white lotuses were tied with blades of *arukai*, the holy grass, and with copper-colored *nandi* leaves. He wore a silk garment still damp after his ritual bath. His chest was painted with fretworks of sandal paste scented with *kôttam*. Normally he loved the acrid smell of smoke rising from the honey, milk, and sugar burned in a ritual fire. Usually till midday he moved between the steps to the river and the shrines of the gods and the temples where the *Vedas* are read. He went home after noon, his parasol open, carrying his staff, his water jar, his dry fire-sticks, and leaves of *kusha*, the sacred grass. He constantly muttered verses from the *Vedas*. A sacred thread could be seen across his chest. He performed all the rituals, never transgressing any rule set down in the holy books. He knew how to kindle the sacred fire in the way that Brahmâ himself had established.

The second genie belonged to the order of knights. He always dressed smartly. Loaded with ornaments of faultless stones, he wore a royal crown. His tuft was tied with chains of champak, *karuvilai*, and red convolvulus, fresh and fragrant water lilies, rattan, and other plants. His garland was composed of rare flowers linked by strings of jewels. Brilliant rings sparkled on his fingers. His broad chest had the sheen of *kumkuma* flowers. His loins were wrapped in a vivid garment of thick red silk. Among many delicacies brought on gold platters for him to eat was strongly spiced Shâli rice. His whole body was coral red. He ruled over the sea-encircled world, and held in his hands a war drum, a white parasol, feather fans, a waving pennant, an elephant hook, a spear, and metal chains. He had repulsed attacks by countless kings renowned for their bravery. Having conquered the world, he ruled it with justice, punished evildoers, and protected the world like a new Vishnu. His fame spread further every day.

The good genie of the illustrious merchant order had the sheen of pure gold. He wore most of the attributes of an invincible monarch except the crown. He cared for the comforts of the citizens, as becomes a merchant. His symbols were a pair of scales and a plough. His dress, admired by all, was made of fine brocade. His tuft was tied with a garland of red ixora, *tâlai*, honey-laden lotus, night jasmine, white lilies, red cotton, and myrobalan. His torso, resembling a thunderbolt, was painted with a sandal paste that glowed like burnished gold. He often gave, or attended, elaborate dinners consisting of chick-peas, green peas, black peas, lentils, and several kinds of beans. He took his meal before midday, holding water in the cup of his hand. Then he visited all the granaries where the rice stocks are stored, the fields full of birds, and the shops, before resting in the fragrant shade of the river portias. He carried in his hands shining cymbals and a melodious harp. He seemed to exude wealth; and he honored his guests. He sold to any who wanted them the rarest goods from the mountains or the sea. When he chose to, he could look like a peasant, dedicated to the innocent task of making the soil fructify; he resembled Shiva, the god who wears the crescent moon in his thick matted hair.

Then appeared the guardian genie of the craftsmen, worshiped with great honors in the industrious city of Madurai. His complexion was that of the *karuvilai* flower. He wore ornaments of silver and a brightly colored loincloth. His broad chest had been rubbed with dry paste of fragrant *ahil*. He wore a crown made of flowers taken from trees, creepers, ponds, and wild shrubs. His hoe had been wrought by the best ironsmith. He was esteemed by all the citizens. His body resembled a well-polished sapphire. His garment was splendid. He knew the art of dance and the various modes of music.

The four genii now spoke to one another:

"For ages we have known that this unfortunate city was doomed and would be burned the day its king should fail in rendering justice. The time has come when we must go." They had already left their respective districts before the brave Kannaki had torn away her breast.

The wide street of the grain merchants, the festooned street of the temple carts, and the four streets where the four castes lived were as filled with tumult as on the day when Arjuna, a monkey on his flag, started the fire that burned the forest of Kândâ. The flames avoided the homes of virtuous men, but destroyed the abodes of dishonest people and impostors. Cows and calves could escape unharmed into the broad street where pious cowherds lived. Fierce elephants with their females, and horses, ran swiftly beyond the city walls.

The flames awoke women asleep on their soft beds, drunk with wine and pleasure beside their men, their young breasts well massaged with creams, their eyes darkened with collyrium, their hair adorned with opening buds that made the air smell of honey. Pollen fell on nipples reddened with *kumkuma* and breasts adorned with strings of pearls. Children, lisping with rosy lips, awoke on their small beds. They ran out, faltering, holding their mothers' hands, followed by old women with gray hair. Mothers who had not failed in their duty and had honored their guests rejoiced and praised the god of Fire who, with a thousand tongues, rose high into the sky. They said:

"This woman lost her man who wore a rich necklace, but she gained victory with her golden ankle bracelet. The upheaval her breast has created is fully justified."

Dancing girls ran away from blazing theatres. In the well-known street of the musicians, expert in the sixty-four arts, the din of drums, the soft sound of the flute, the poignant voice of the harp, could no longer be heard. All asked:

"Where has this woman come from? Where was she born? By what magic could she—alone and mourning her husband, by the power alone of an ankle bracelet—burn our city and defeat an irresponsible monarch?"

The city was deprived of all evening ceremonies, of Vedic hymns, of sacrificial fires, of all worship, of the ritual where the lamps are lit. There was silence that night. No sound of drums was heard. Unable to bear the heat of the flames, the goddess of the town appeared near the heroic woman, oppressed by her boundless sorrow. Her heart bruised by the loss of her husband, Kannaki wandered, wailing, through the lanes and streets, faltering, stupefied, unconscious of events.

The goddess of Madurai came
before Kannaki, who had torn away
her lovely youthful breast,
but equaled in her power
the power of Lakshmî (Fortune),
of Sarasvatî (Knowledge), and of Kâlî (Time),
who stands upon the body of the buffalo-king.

⚜ CANTO TWENTY-THREE ⚜

The Explanation

Katturaikâdai

The great goddess of Madurai was the protector of the royal clan that rules over the cool port of Korkai, the Cape of the Virgin, and Mount Podiyil. Her power extends as far as the Himalaya.

The goddess wears the moon's crescent in her thick, tangled hair. Her eyes resemble lotuses. Her face is luminous. Her coral lips cover gleaming teeth. Her body is blue on the left side and golden on the right. She carries a gold lotus in her left hand, and in her right a sparkling and fearsome sword. The victors' circlet can be seen on her left ankle; another unrivaled anklet tinkles on her right.

Not daring to come too near the beautiful woman whom adversity had so cruelly smitten and who in her despair had torn away her own breast, the wise goddess approached her from behind and gently said:

"Blessed woman! Can you listen to my request?"

Kannaki, whose face was shriveled with pain, turned toward her and said:

"Who are you? Why do you follow me? Can you fathom the depth of my sorrow?"

The goddess of Madurai replied:

"I know the immensity of your pain. Faultless woman! I am the tutelar deity of this vast city. Anxious for your husband's future, I wish to speak to you. Listen to what I say, woman with the golden bracelets. Noble woman! As a friend, I ask your attention to the great tragedy that is breaking my heart. Dear one! Listen to the sad tale of the misdeeds committed by our kings in their previous incarnations. Listen to your husband's past life, cause of all the evils that have overwhelmed us.

"Until this day my ears have heard only the chant of the *Vedas*, never the tolling of the bell of justice. We have seen the people mock at monarchs come to pay tribute and bow down before our king, whose edicts were never questioned by his subjects. It is true that young girls with timid looks inspire in him, on occasion, passions that he cannot control, like a young elephant that escapes from his mahout. But there can be no wrong in this for a young prince who is the scion of a noble and virtuous clan.

"Do you know the story of the Pândya monarch who with his own hands broke the diadem and glowing bracelets of heaven's king, though he was armed with thunderbolts? One day this Pândya was walking near the cottage of a man named Kîrandai, whose life had no value for anyone. He heard the wife of this poor man say, 'You want to go away, leaving me in this open yard, and you say that no door can protect us better than the royal justice. Is our door rotten, then?' The king closed both his ears as if a red-hot iron had pierced him through and through. He shuddered with fear; his heart was afire. He cut off his own hand so that his scepter might be strengthened. Since then the name of the whole dynasty has remained untarnished.

"Another king, who handled his polished spear with great art, and fed his soldiers generously after bringing peace and order to the land, one day assembled his subjects in the audience hall. A most learned Brahmin named Parâshar had heard of the magnificence of this Chêra, who, it was said, had with his saber opened the gateway of heaven before a great Tamil poet of Brahmin blood. Parâshar thought: I must go to meet this Chêra, renowned for his valor and the power of his lance. This Brahmin was born in the peace-loving and fertile country of Puhâr, whose kings bear a virtuous scepter and a victorious sword. You know that one of them gave his own flesh to save a humble dove, and that another avenged a cow that had been wronged. Parâshar set out on his journey. He passed through the hills of Malaya, deep jungles, countless villages and cities. He was a great master of dialectics, an art greatly appreciated by the twice-born, who, seeking unity with infinite good, light the three sacred fires ordained by the four *Vedas*, perform the five rituals of sacrifice, and never fail in the six duties of a priest.

"Parâshar defeated all opponents in philosophical debates and thus won from the king the title of *Pârpanavâhai*, Sublime Scholar. As he was returning homeward, laden with gifts, he reached the village of Tangâl, in the Pândya kingdom, where noble Brahmins lived. In this village there was a green *bodhi* tree. Tired, the traveler, with his staff, his bowl, his white parasol, his five sticks, his bundle, and his shoes, rested awhile. He said, 'Long live the conqueror whose immaculate parasol so well protects his subjects and whose realm is secure! Long live the protector of men who dragged the *kadamba* tree from the sea! Long live the king who carved his name on the proud brow of the Himalaya! Long live the royal *Poraiyan* who rules over the plains where the cool and lovely Porunai flows. Long live the great King Mândaran Chêral!'

"Laughing children crowded about him. Some had long curls; others already had their hair in tufts. Several could still hardly speak with their coral lips. They all came to play on the road. Parâshar said to them, 'Young Brahmins! If you can faultlessly repeat after me the Vedic hymns I shall chant, you may take my bundle, which contains a treasure.' Then Alamar Shelvan, young son of the renowned priest Vârttikan, stood forth. His red lips still tasted of his mother's milk. Lisping, before all his playmates, he proudly repeated the sacred words without an error. Charmed by this child of the south, the old Brahmin gave him a string of pearls, brilliant gems, gold bracelets and earrings. Then he continued his journey.

"Some policemen of the town, jealous of Vârttikan, whose son went decked in these ornaments, accused him: 'This Brahmin appropriated some treasure that he found, which, by law, belongs to the king.' They threw him into prison. Vârttikan's wife Kârttikai became mad with despair. In her sorrow, she wallowed in the dust, shrieking and cursing everybody. Seeing her, the goddess Durgâ, whose name is ever untarnished, refused to let the door of her temple be opened at prayer time. The king, whose sword is ever victorious, heard that the heavy door of the temple would not open. He was dismayed, and called his ministers: 'Some injustice must have been done. Let me know if you have noticed some unconscious failure in the discharge of our duties toward the goddess who gives victory.'

"His young messengers bowed before his feet and told him about Vârttikan. 'This is unfair!' cried the king in anger. Summoning Vârttikan to him, he said, 'Your duty is to forgive us. My virtuous rule has not yet ended, although, through the fault of my servants, I have been led astray from the path of justice.' And the king gave him the country of Tangâl, with its rice fields watered by irrigation channels from the lakes. He also offered him the town of Vayalûr and its immense income. Then he lay prostrate at the feet of Kârttikai's husband to pacify his anger.

"And the door of the temple, abode of the goddess who rides a deer, opened with a crash that echoed through all the ancient city's streets, lined by clifflike mansions. Then the king sent a drummer on an elephant through the streets to proclaim his order: 'All prisoners shall be reprieved, all unpaid taxes remitted. Those who discover a treasure may enjoy their fortune in peace.'

"Now I shall explain how our king could be led to such injustice. It was predicted long ago that great Madurai would be burned and its king would be made destitute during the month of Adi, the eighth day after the full moon appeared on a Friday, at a time when the Pleiades and Aries should be in the ascendant.

"Listen, woman with the rich bracelets! Once the kings Vasu and Kumâra, who with their shining swords and strong armies had justly ruled the richly forested Kalinga country, became enemies. One ruled over Singapuram in the plain; the other over Kapilapuram in the bamboo forest. They belonged to a great dynasty whose fortune appeared everlasting. While they were fighting, no one dared to approach within six miles of the battlefield.

"A young merchant named Sangaman, anxious to increase his wealth, came with his wife in the garb of a refugee. He carried a huge bale on his head and soon began to sell his precious wares in a bazaar in Singapuram.

"Woman with gold bracelets! Your husband Kôva-lan, in a previous incarnation, was known as Bharata. He was in the service of valorous King Vasu. He had renounced his vow of nonviolence and was hated by all. He believed Sangaman to be a spy of the enemy king. He had him caught, brought him before the king of the victorious lance, and caused him to be beheaded. Nîli, the wife of the unhappy Sangaman, found herself left alone. She ran through the streets and squares, creating great uproar and shouting, 'King, is that your justice? Merchants, is that justice? Workmen, do you call that justice?' For fourteen days she wandered, taking no rest; then, inspired by the thought that the day was auspicious, she climbed the high rocks to follow her husband in death. As she threw herself down into the valley, she shouted a curse: 'He who inflicted a cruel death upon my husband shall share his fate.' So today a destiny that no power could stop has brought you this ordeal.

"Hearken to what I say! Actions committed in past lives always bear fruit. No amount of austerity or virtue can loose the bonds of our actions. Woman with lovely hair! After fourteen days you shall see the man you love in his celestial garb, for never more can you behold his human form."

When she had thus explained to Kannaki—soon herself to become a goddess—all the strange events of the day, the goddess of Madurai was able to control the flames that were devouring the city.

Then Kannaki told her:

"I wish neither to sit nor sleep nor stop, until I see the husband dear to my heart." She went and broke all her bracelets, as widows do, in the temple of Durgâ. She cried, "I entered this city through the eastern gate with a beloved husband. Today I leave it through the western portal, alone." Unaware of light or darkness, she wandered, desolate, near the Vaigai in flood. Sad and distracted, unheeding when she fell in a ditch or climbed a cliff, she ascended the sacred hill where the god Neduvêl resides, he whose fiery lance once tore through the entrails of the sea. There, under the kinos in bloom, Kannaki wept and lamented: "Alas, I am guilty of a great crime."

Fourteen days thus passed. Then heaven's king, with all his angels, thought the time had come to proclaim the saintliness of this woman, whose name men shall ever recall. He showered down a rain of never-fading flowers, then appeared and bowed at her feet.

On a divine chariot, seated beside Kôvalan, who had been put to death in the royal city, Kannaki, with her hair profuse as a forest, ascended, happy, into heaven.

CODA

Even the gods pay honor to the wife
who worships no one save her husband.
Kannaki, pearl among all women of the earth,
is now a goddess, and is highly honored
by all the gods who dwell in Paradise.

EPILOGUE

Thus ends the book of Madurai, which has depicted the virtues, the victories, and the great deeds of the Pândya monarch, whose lance won the greatest fame among the three kings who rule the three kingdoms.

This book has described an ancient and famous city, the splendor of its feasts, the genii of the town, the happiness and prosperity of village folk, the fertility produced by the river Vaigai and the rains faithfully brought by heavy clouds in the proper season.

This book has shown the two kinds of drama (*virutti*), the human tragedy (*ârapati*) and the mythological play (*shâttuvadi*), accompanied by songs and dances. It also contains a eulogy of the virtuous Pândya monarch, the noble Nedunjeliyan, who defeated the northern Aryans and established peace among the Tamils at the southermost end of the peninsula, and who died, seated on his throne, as if asleep, beside his queen of never-questioned virtue.

BOOK THREE

The Book of Vanji

The Dance of the Mountain Girls

Kunrakkuravai

The mountain girls sang:

"We came to the mountain's green groves,
running after swift birds, chasing green parrots.
We came to bathe in the cool streams and springs.
Mirthful, we wished to play.

"We met a lady and asked her:
" 'Lovely lady, standing under the fragrant *vengai*
tree of our mountain, whence have you come? How did
you lose one breast? Looking at you, we shudder as if
from fear.'
"She calmly answered:
" 'I am a pitiable woman. A merciless fate took away
my husband on that ill-fated day when gay Madurai and
its noble king perished in a great fire.'"
The mountain girls were stunned with awe. Folding
their hands, under the bright tinkling bangles of their
wrists, they bowed down before the poor woman. Flowers rained from the sky.

"We stood astounded beside our men while the gods took her away with her husband. Never before had a goddess come to our village. Hunters, dwelling in huts in the forest! Today we shall proclaim her our tutelar deity. Village hunters! Let us build an altar in the cool shade of the fragrant *vengai*, on the hillside where the waterfalls sing. Forest folk! We shall accept her as our goddess! Sound the great drums! Strike tambourines and blow the conch! Ring bells, while we sing our mountain songs. We shall offer her incense and spices, bring her flowers, and erect a wall with a door. We shall chant prayers and throw flower petals for the lady who lost her breast, that peace and prosperity may come to our great mountain forever."

PRELUDE

Kolucchol

Beloved and bejeweled lady, look at us
and you will see the shimmering
of waterfalls and singing brooks
brighter than heaven's bow. The clear
waters appear as black as collyrium,
yellow as orpiment, redder
than pure vermilion. And we
shall bathe and swim in every stream.

The mountain prince jeered at our innocence.
He told us, "Do not fear," and went away.
But we shall bathe now in the stream
that springs forth from the hill
far hidden in the forest's depths.
Be careful! For a stream in spate
may be already pregnant
from the lustful rocks' embraces.

We shall play in the cool river
that cruel mountain rocks
have raped before it reached us.
We feel no jealousy when other girls
bathe in cool streams that have
caressed our mountain prince. We are
not envious of ebullient cascades
that bring the precious gold dust down.
But we feel jealous when strange girls
court them and long for their caress.

Why should we deem it an offense
when an unconscious rivulet
brings us the flowers of the hills?
We play with the innocent stream
that yields us up its garlands.
We want no other lover.

VERSE INTERLUDE

Pâttumadai

O charming babbling girl!
We bathed and played in holy streams
till our collyrium-painted eyes grew red.
Now let us pray to handsome Murugan,
who bears a vigorous never-straying staff.
For him we dance the dance of love.
Come, let us sing for him, my lovely friends!

We worship the unfailing lance
of that divinity who forever dwells
in shrines at Chendil, Chengôdu, and Erakam,
and in the temple on the high white hill.

His leaf-shaped lance once pierced
a demon masquerading as a mango tree.
He followed after, even to the depths
of the great world-englobing sea.
In his twelve hands this six-faced god
carries his lance, and riding a peacock
he brandishes the proud weapon
that could check the demons' conquests.

Even the king of the heavenly hosts
sings his prowess when he fights the genii,
defeating their strong armies.
A lance looks beautiful if brandished deftly
in the hands of him six mothers fed
upon a lotus bed among the reeds—
a lance that clove the heron rock and split
the broad chest of a demon
who had sought refuge there.

ANOTHER INTERLUDE

Good girls with rich bracelets!
My mother makes me laugh.
She thinks I am possessed
by the handsome god Murugan.
She called an exorcist, not noticing
what all the village talks about.
My illness sprang from love alone,
and from a prince, and a cool hill
where pepper grows.

Good girls with bright bangles!
I had a good laugh when the exorcist
said he could heal the curious malady
a mountain prince has caused.

This man is hopelessly obtuse.
And if the god who clove
the sacred heron rock
obeys an exorcist like him,
he must be rather dull himself.

Good girls with heavy bracelets!
I laughed aloud when the exorcist
tried words to cure my malady—
gift of a prince and of a fragrant hill.
This man has lost his wits.
And if the son of Shiva,
who sits beneath a holy tree,
obeys him and appears before us,
he is not too clever himself.

Graceful girls, preciously adorned!
Really one has to laugh
when an exorcist attempts
to cure the lovely malady
caused by embraces of a mountain prince.
He seems to be a bit naïve.
And if the god who's garlanded
in rice shoots and in winter blooms
appears before us, he's as foolish
as the exorcist who tries to cure me thus.

ANOTHER INTERLUDE

The son of the god Shiva lives under a banyan tree
with a goddess all bedecked in jewelry.
He will come, riding on his peacock,
to our country when the family magician
performs his rites of exorcism.

When he arrives, we shall ask him to bless
our lovemaking with the handsome mountain prince.

Son of the god who lives on Mount Kailâsa!
We worship the feet of your wife,
fair as an *ashoka* in bloom.
Like us, she is a daughter of the hills.
Her forehead, blue as the peacock,
is like a young and crescent moon.
We pray that she may intercede,
obtain for us, in lieu of marriage,
abduction in a hero's arms.

We worship your beautiful feet,
son of the daughter of the hills
who wears *valli* flowers
over her moon-crescent brow.
She is a daughter of the Kaurava
who dwell on our massive mountain.
God, give me as husband a man whose fame
will spread across the world.
Your wife is a Kaurava girl,
a daughter of our tribe.
We worship your feet, O six-faced god!
May he who promised marriage to me,
his hand upon the feet of your image,
be willing that a legal bond
replace our furtive pleasures.

ANOTHER INTERLUDE

While we sang hymns to honor Murugan,
the mountain prince, bedecked in wreaths
of choicest flowers, was hiding not far off

and listening to us cunningly.
When songs were over, I went straight to him;
I touched his feet and stood before him.
Friend, blessed by all the gods, do you know
what I said? I told him honestly:
"You came one day to our village
with your lance and your garland of *kadamba* flowers
in search of some attractive girl.
You imagined we should take you for Murugan?
But you do not have six faces,
and you don't come riding on a peacock.
You don't have the god's broad shoulders,
and Valli, the Kauravas' daughter,
stands not at your side.
The simple villagers are not so innocent
as to mistake you for the god
to whom *kadamba* flowers are dear."
He listened, mute, to everything I said
about the village gossip and our furtive love;
and went away, leaving my heart heavy with pain.
Will the mountain prince marry me?

ANOTHER INTERLUDE

Let's sing the praises of the virtuous girl
whose torn-off breast could burn Madurai down.
Heaven and Earth are shaken by her will.
The gods themselves came down to seek her man.
Sing! Dance! Lucky friend, sing!
Sing! Dance! Lucky friend, sing!

We sing the glory of a girl
who burned that great city and its palaces
whose banners rose high in the sky

the day the wheel of justice crashed.
And while we sing the praises of the girl
who brought Madurai low, we'll ask a favor:
"Grant us as a lawful husband
the prince of our mountains."

Virtuous women, come to worship
the lovely Kannaki, with pubis like
a cobra's hood — she who once stood
smiling amid our fertile fields.
When they restored her dear husband
to this loveliest of women,
the gods all praised her greatly.

All heaven's gods did honor
to this lady in the forest where she stood
under the shadow of the kinos.
They lifted her to heaven's great city
from which no one returns.
And if we sing the praises of this girl
who'll not return, we may obtain
that all our village folk may share her fate.
Our hamlet is particularly blessed,
for it will see the marriage
of the handsome hill prince
and a girl adorned with golden bangles.

While we were singing our songs and dancing the dance
of love, our lover, attracted by the sound, appeared.

May the prince of the western hills, who carved the
bow, his proud emblem, on the Himalaya, and who rules
over our mountains, drink the cup of heroes and live for
many days in constant happiness.

The Choice of a Stone

Kâtchikkâdai

In the illustrious lineage of the Chêras a mighty hero named Shenguttuvan was born. To the wonderment of the gods, his sword captured the Kadambu kingdom entrenched behind the sea. Later, unchallenged, he led his army to carve the bow, proud symbol of his dynasty, upon the brow of the Himalaya.

One day Shenguttuvan was resting near a fountain in his silver palace, with his queen, Ilangô Vênmâl, at his side, when he suddenly felt a desire to visit the mountains, to see the tall forest crested with clouds, and to hear the waterfalls roaring like beaten drums.

He left Vanji, followed by a crowd of women and retainers who trailed along the road for many leagues. On his tall elephant, he looked like heaven's king, accompanied by celestial nymphs, setting off for a picnic in the gardens of Paradise filled with magic flowers. The royal party passed through country where trees were covered with flowers of gold. The rivers had broad sandy banks. In midstream there were islands with groves of tender trees and murmuring springs of fresh water. It seemed as if the city of Indra, with its dancing girls and its assemblies, were following the royal progress.

King Shenguttuvan reached the white sand dunes of the river Periyar, which rushed down from the hills in cascades that resembled a silver necklace on the chest of Vishnu. Its waters were strewn with flower petals fallen from cottonwood trees, kinos, laburnums, gamboges, and sweet-scented sandal. Swarms of bees and insects buzzed charmingly about. The royal party stopped near the stream to rest.

Hill women approached, singing and dancing as is their custom, while their priests chanted hymns to the god who bears a red lance. The songs of harvesters, the rhythmic sound of flails, the shouts of field wardens, the cries of forest men searching for honeycombs, the noise of drums, the roar of waterfalls, the trumpeting of elephants attacking tigers, the piercing shrieks of bird-chasers hidden in their shelters, the cries of the mahouts driving wild elephants toward their traps—all these sounds blended with the clamor of the marching host.

Tribal chiefs approached, resembling defeated kings come to pay homage, laden with rare presents for the court of Vanji. They brought ivory, sandalwood, whisks of stag hair, honey, precious woods, vermilion, eye-black, yellow orpiment, cardamom, pepper, and flour of arrowroot. They offered ripe millet, large coconuts, delicate mangoes, leaf-garlands, breadfruit, garlic, sugar cane, creepers in bloom, bunches of areca nuts, palm leaves, delicious bananas, small tigers, baby lions, young elephants, monkeys, bears, mountain hinds, timid deer with their fawns, musk deer, shy mongooses, brilliant peacocks, wildcats, chickens, and sweet-spoken parrots.

They said to the king:

"For six generations we have been your vassals. May your glory last forever. In the forest, under a striped kino, a woman, with a breast torn off, appeared to be suffering an unspeakable agony. Later, honored by the gods, she rose into the sky. We do not know whence she came, whose daughter she was. Coming from some other land, she entered your kingdom. May your illustrious line be continued for centuries."

Shâttan, the famous poet, who had watched this scene with keen interest, said to the king who bears a long spear and on whom the joy of the world rests:

"Noble and mighty ruler, hear me! I can tell you the strange story of that woman of the bright golden bangles, and of her dear husband. I can explain all the events that occurred and how a precious ankle bracelet brought ill luck. I can also relate how this splendid woman chose to plead her own case before a king, leader of great armies, and how the whole city of Madurai was destroyed by a fire born of the young breast of this goddess of Faithfulness. Throwing her gold anklet at the feet of the queen, she cried in her fury: 'Woman with the five plaits! You shall be blown away by the storm of my rage.'

"The Pândya king, on whose broad chest the goddess of Fortune often rested, was seated on his lion-throne. He staggered, fainted, and fell dead. The queen thought: 'The king could not bear to hear of the ordeal suffered by this woman with the long, flower-entwined hair.' She did not feel hurt by Kannaki's words. She did not feel any illness. But she fell at the lotus feet of her lord. Unable to bear her sorrow, she died, saying: 'I must follow my king.'

"It may be that it was the intention of this woman to inform you, illustrious monarch, of the great injustice that the mighty Pândya had committed. Refusing to return to the land of her birth, she entered your kingdom. May your reign and glory last till the end of time."

When he heard of the cruel deed of the Pândya, the Chêra king of kings was indignant. He said:

"The noble Pândya king was indeed fortunate to have paid with his life for a most detestable action. For death alone has power to rehabilitate a once virtuous scepter disgraced by merciless destiny. If the rains are late in coming, disaster is at hand. Injustice breeds fear among men. The power of a king is not to be envied. When his soul is noble and he seeks the welfare of his subjects, they complain of his tyranny and reward him by ingratitude."

The king graciously thanked the poet who had conveyed this sad story to him. Then he spoke to his queen:

"A virtuous woman lost her life because her husband died. Another wandered in anger through our kingdom. Charming woman, tell me: in your judgment, which one should we admire?"

Questioned by the monarch, the queen replied:

"May the joys of heaven await the Pândya queen whose soul departed even before she felt the pain of separation from her lord. And may the new goddess of Faithfulness, whose presence sanctifies our kingdom, be forever honored as she deserves to be."

The king, whose parasol is adorned with flowers, approved of her wisdom. Then he turned to his counselors. They suggested:

"To make a proper image of the goddess of Faithfulness, a stone will have to be brought from the immortal mountain, Podiyil, or from the great Himalaya on which the bow, emblem of your clan, was once carved. These two mountains are equal in sacredness, for one is purified by the flow of the Kâverî, the other by the celestial Ganges."

The king answered:

"For a prince of my rank, of what prowess would it be to go choose a stone from Mount Podiyil to bathe it in the Kâverî? On the Himalaya, king of all mountains, there dwell twice-born Brahmins and sages with long matted hair, with garments never dry from ritual bathing, and with chests adorned by the three-threaded cord. They wield untold powers derived from the three fires they feed with offerings. Should the king of mountains refuse to give up the stone we need to carve a beautiful image of the goddess of Faithfulness, we will leave our country, wearing a wreath of wild fig leaves, and we will demonstrate the precariousness of their lives to the evil men who dared survive our former massacres. We will climb the high peak of the Himalaya who gave his ever-youthful daughter to the god Shiva, he who wears the moon on his forehead. Many were the suitors who courted the daughter of the king of mountains. He refused her to all. We will launch our attack against this northern king. We will cleave asunder his mighty crown on which the rays of the nocturnal planet gleam. We will fell all trees that dare cast flowers of kino or *mandâra* at his feet. We will wrest from his neck the wreath of victory."

With these proud words, the king ordered that, to celebrate the day, garlands of fig leaves be brought for all his soldiers, fierce as war elephants, and that the royal parasol be carried round in a procession.

There are several wreaths of fig leaves, all emblems of victory. One is used to recall the suzerainty of the Chêra. Another is worn to commemorate their establishment as kings of kings. A third recalls their ability to feed large rations to their brave soldiers. A fourth is used on anniversaries of the sacking of foreign cities. The last one is worn after battle when the victory song is sung on enemy territory.

The king soon ordered the army to put on its battle array and wear fresh garlands of palm leaves. He then addressed the troops:

"Before the walls of our golden city, ever young, we shall wear wreaths of new flowers plucked from wild fig trees. These wreaths shall be the only sweethearts of our swords till we return."

The chief minister, Villavan-kôdai, answered for all:

"May your virtuous rule last for many years! On the blood-drenched battlefield of Konkan, you bravely fought your adversaries till they had to surrender their standards bearing the emblems of the tiger and the fish. The fame of these great deeds has already spread to the four corners of the earth that eight celestial elephants support. Never shall I forget the sight of your war elephant advancing in the midst of the Tamil legions which had destroyed the assembled armies of Konkanars, Kalinjars, cruel Karunâtars, Bengalars, Gangars, Kattiyars, and Aryans from the north.

"Never shall we forget the courage you showed when, with the pious purpose of bringing your mother to bathe in the furious waters of the Ganges in flood, you fought alone against several thousand Aryans, so fiercely that the god of Death was stunned, and stood as motionless as a stone.

"No one can stop you if you choose to impose Tamil rule over the whole sea-encircled world. Send your message to the northern countries: 'The great king advances toward the north to bring back a Himalayan stone in which the image of a god is to be carved.' Let the message bear your own baked-clay seal on which are shown the bow, the fish, the tiger-head, all royal emblems of the Tamil kings, and be dispatched to all northern monarchs."

The ruler of Alumbil then suggested:

"All the kings of this rosewood continent maintain spies in Vanji, your great capital. They will themselves dispatch the news to their own kings, famous for their richly caparisoned war elephants. We need only announce your expedition, to the sound of drums, throughout the city."

The king, whose army is invincible, gave his approval. As soon as he returned to the glorious city whose wealth, increased by the booty acquired in countless wars, has never known decline, a drummer perched on a tall elephant proclaimed the edict through the town:

"Long live our gracious king! May he protect the world for centuries to come. The king will set out for the Himalaya, on which his seal, the bow, is already carved, to bring back a stone. All kings of the north must submit and bring him their tribute, recalling the great deeds of him who conquered Kadambu beyond the sea, and who carved his emblem on the glorious brow of the Himalaya. Let them either heed this suggestion or abandon sons and wives and retire to live as hermits in the forest. Long live the vanguard of the troops, dearer than his own eyes to the valorous king who wears on his ankle the golden circlet of victory!"

⚬⚬ CANTO TWENTY-SIX ⚬⚬

Bringing Back the Great Stone

Kâlkôtkâdai

When the drum was sounded, the king arose and mounted to the throne of his ancestors. The high priest, the chief astrologer, the royal ministers, and the army commanders approached. First they acclaimed the monarch, calling him king of kings. Then they asked for his instructions about the march to the north.

The Chêra, whose white parasol is borne higher than those of other kings, thus made proclamation:

"It would be unworthy of us to let pass unnoticed the disrespectful talk of these few northern kings – talk reported to me by some sages who came to our land in pilgrimage from the Himalaya. I therefore call on the gods to lead my own people to their doom if ever my unfailing sword is unable to sow terror in our enemies' camps and in their leaders' warlike hearts, and to compel their kings to bring down to us, carrying it on their very crowns, the great stone in which we will carve the image of our beloved goddess."

The high priest counseled him:

"Mighty victor in many a hard battle, your proclamation can apply only to the Chôla and the Pândya, who wear garlands of fig leaves and margosa and adorn their heads with precious crowns. No king of the northern lands dares face the storm of your anger. None could wish to offend you. Therefore, appease your wrath."

Next came the chief astrologer, who possessed all the secrets of the stars' mysterious power. He knew the planet that rules each day, the hour of the stars' conjunctions, and the effect of the zodiac on the lives of men. He rose and said:

"Noble and mighty monarch! Be firm in your resolve, for the hour is auspicious! You can compel all the kings of the world to bow down before your lotus feet. Do not delay, but start in the direction on which your mind is set."

As soon as he heard this oracle, the king ordered that his sword and parasol be borne ahead of him toward the north. The din of the big war drums and the cheers of the soldiers burst forth so deafeningly that the great snake who bears the world had to lower his head. Lamps set with rubies dispelled the darkness of the night. Banners waved in the wind. The army, eager to destroy the enemy, joined the members of the five assemblies, the priests, the tax gatherers, and all the administrators of this land rich in swift stallions and towering war elephants, in a mighty cheer: "Long live the ruler of the world!"

The royal sword, terror of men, and the white parasol were carried off on a tall elephant, fed by attendants with enormous balls of rice. They were borne to a chosen camp site beyond the city walls. The king, distinguished by his wreath of palm leaves and wild fig flowers, entered the great hall of audience, where he offered a banquet to the army commanders, exalted by the prospect of carnage.

The king adorned his crown with rare jewels and fig leaves from Vanji, the town that bears the fig tree's name. Meanwhile the morning drums were sounded at the city gates to warn all the kings of the world that the time had come to bow down before the Tamil power.

Within the wreath of fig leaves, symbol of victory, the king placed on his head the sandal of Shiva, upon whom the world rests, and who wears in his tangled hair the crescent of the moon. The king, who never bowed down before a man, made the circuit of the temple and then prostrated himself before the image of the god. The flowers of his wreath faded in the dense smoke that arose from the ritual fires ceaselessly fed by the temple priests. And then at last he mounted his war elephant and departed.

Brahmins, with offerings from the temple of Adakamâdam where the god Vishnu sleeps in yogic trance, drew near and blessed the king: "May victory ever follow in the path of Kuttunâdu's king, lord of the western land." Since he was already wearing in his crown the sandal of the god in whose tangled hair the Ganges is born, he placed the offerings of this other divinity on his handsome shoulder, loaded with splendid ornaments.

As he rode away in majesty and magnificence, the dancers from all the theatres came and lined his path. With arms crossed, they cried: "Triumphant king! Seated under your parasol on your war elephant loaded with garlands of palms and lianas, your grace so troubles our hearts that our bangles fall from our arms."

At his side went the Magadha poets, panegyrists, and bards, proclaiming his mighty deeds on many battle-fields, while elephant drivers, horsemen, and foot soldiers with their flashing swords shouted praises of the royal spear's great prowess.

Passing before Vanji, his capital, the monarch resembled Indra, the ruler of heaven, setting out from the celestial city to attack an army of nefarious genii. The army, with its commanding staff and its van, seemed to cover the whole sea-girt land. Under its weight the spines of the mountains bent and the plains shook. The king rode in advance of impetuous cavalry and brightly colored chariots. Soon they neared the Blue Mountain, the Nîla-Giri. There, while the fierce elephants swung their trunks angrily, the charioteers, the horses, the hardy soldiers, encamped for the night, protected by their sentinels. The king, more brilliant than the sun, granted Earth the favor of placing his foot upon her face. Then, withdrawing into his tent, he received the homage of his valiant troops.

Inspired by a desire to see the master of the world, of a splendor equal to that of heaven's king, some sages, traveling through mid-air, appeared before the royal council tent. Their bodies shone like lightning-bolts.

The king welcomed them with respect. They said to him: "Hear us, Chêra king, born in glorious Vanji by the grace of Shiva, the god with tangled hair. We are on holy pilgrimage to the Malaya hills where learned Brahmins dwell. To protect them is your sacred duty." They gave him their blessings and departed.

Then came dancers from Konkana in the Mysore country. They cried: "Long live the ruler of the sea-encircled world!" These wild Karunâtars wore the picturesque dress of their country. The girls had twined lustrous garlands in their long black wavy hair. Their young breasts were adorned with golden chains. Their long eyes were curved like a graceful carp. They sang a summer song that pictured their longing:

> "When the blackbird starts his song,
> above the humming of the bees,
> so like the murmur of a harp,
> then summer comes, the buds burst out,
> and we—we long for lovers' arms."

A delegation came also from Kudagu, another part of the Chêra empire, bringing dancing girls with rich bracelets and rolling carp-shaped eyes. These sang a love song to the theme of a winter dance:

> "Lady with elaborate armlets,
> arrayed in all your finest gems,
> look at the clouds that war against
> each other with swift lightning-bolts!
> His dangerous mission done, my love
> has sped back to me in his hurtling car."

Members of the Ôvar tribe came too, blessing the monarch thus: "May the king, whose sword is ever powerful, lead his expedition to triumph. May he live for all time, and may friends, panegyrists, and courtiers flourish in his palace."

The king, before whose lance all enemies tremble, gave rewards to those who sang his praises—to each in fitting degree as suggested by the lord of ceremonies and pageants. He lavished many precious jewels on them.

As the king was resting in his tent, a guard reported:

"Great king, bearer of a righteous scepter, on whose standard a bow appears! Led by Sanjayan, there have just approached your camp, coming from the northern kingdoms, two hundred dancing girls, two hundred and eight musicians, a hundred jugglers excelling in the ninety-six forms of illusionism, a hundred large war cars, five hundred joyful elephants, ten thousand horses with cropped manes, twenty thousand chariots loaded with bales of gifts with a picture on each parcel showing the nature of its contents, and one thousand brilliantly dressed *kanjuka*, boy prostitutes with long carefully burnished hair."

The king said:

"Bring in Sanjayan and the officeholders, together with the dancing girls and the players of instruments."

Sanjayan was ushered into the splendid tent of the noblest of kings. He bowed low and praised him with great art; he presented the main officeholders and the two hundred musicians. Then he said:

"King, bearer of a most virtuous scepter! Prince Nûrruvar Kannar, through whose country the Ganges flows, sends you the most friendly greetings and this message: 'If the purpose of the Chêra's expedition is to carry back a stone in which an image will be carved, we can wrest from the proud Himalaya a great rock that we shall with our own hands bathe in the Ganges and personally bring to him. It would be a pleasure to undertake such tasks on his behalf.' May you rule forever over the sea-encircled world."

The king, whose army, vast as the ocean, could devour all rival kings and their lethal spears, answered:

"Two sons of Bâla-Kumâra, named Kanaka and Vijaya, together with some other inconsequent northern princes who talk more than they should, made during a banquet some disparaging remarks about the Tamil kings, forgetting our great deeds. Our mighty army, embodiment of death, shall carry its fury to the north. Take our message to Nûrruvar Kannar, and bid him prepare a large fleet of barges and boats so that the army may cross the holy Ganges without delay."

When Sanjayan was gone, the thousand fine-spoken ephebes presented the king with pieces of sandalwood and pearls from the ocean. At that moment the Pândya's rich tribute also arrived. The protector of men ordered the scribes to address to all the kings receipts sealed with the baked-clay imperial seal.

After the messengers had departed with these, the ruler of the sea-girt world received the homage of all the army chiefs. He then broke camp and marched to the Ganges. There the army could cross on the boats prepared by the prudent Kannar, who was on the northern bank to cheer him over. Continuing on, he penetrated into the marshy country of the hostile King Uttara, and marched toward the battlefield.

Uttara, together with Vichitra, Simha, Dhanurdhara, Shiveta, and other northern kings, followed by Kanaka and Vijaya, advanced at the head of an army so vast that it seemed a boundless sea. They said: "We shall test the valor of this Tamil king." Seeing them approach, Shenguttuvan leaped up with joy like a hunting lion who, sick with hunger, sees a herd of elephants. Wearing his garland of portia, he hurled his main forces against the enemy army. Countless standards veiled the sky; the earth trembled with the clamor of taut war drums, strident conchs, clear trumpets, and shrill cymbals. And all the din was penetrated by the deep and noble voice of the fur-covered royal drums, which sounded ready to devour the countless lives offered to them in sacrifice.

The dust that was stirred up—by the feet of the archers marching with their bows on their shoulders, the lancers, the infantry with great shields, the chariots, the carefully led elephants, and the swift horsemen—covered the field with clouds so dense that they jammed the bells hanging from the elephants' necks, and reduced to silence the standard-bearers' conchs, thus preventing them from adding their clamor to the horrendous din of the battle.

The vanguards of the two armies met and struck, and the battle was begun. Severed heads of soldiers went flying, and archers began to pile up the dead. Soldiers whose heads had been cut off stumbled on for a few steps as if dancing to the music of witches with eyes like drumheads. Troops of demonesses ran on to the battlefield to drink the blood gushing from the wounds of the dead and to eat human flesh.

The brave Aryan soldiers, whose chariots had had the reputation of invincibility, were massacred. Their bodies soon piled up on the battlefield. Their chariots were smashed. Their dead elephants and horses were heaped together by the Chêra's order. The king wore his shining armlet, and with great ceremonial placed on his own head a high crown and a wreath of diospyros flowers intertwined with palms. On the field of battle he appeared to the Aryan kings like a new god of Death riding his buffalo and devouring all the living in the span of a day.

Those ablest of lancers, Kanaka and Vijaya, their fearful lances in their hands, together with fifty-two chariot-leaders who had dared speak ill of Tamil kings, were the victims of the anger of King Shenguttuvan. Attempting to escape, some braided their hair like women; others put on monks' robes; others went naked like yogis, rubbing their bodies with ashes; others sat in meditation, as hermits do, with peacock feathers in their hands; some went costumed as minstrels, lutes on their shoulders; others dressed like dancers. Casting aside swords and lances, they ran away in every direction, trembling with fear.

The thickly armored elephants were shaking with terror. Shenguttuvan had them yoked, two by two, like bullocks. Using swords as ploughshares, he dispatched them to crush the enemy as sheaves of wheat are crushed to separate the grain from the straw. Demons ran out to applaud the ploughing up of the field of battle. With long trembling hands, loaded with bracelets, they lifted the crowned heads of dead warriors and placed them in long rows. Then they sang in praise of the god who had first performed the *munrerkkuravai*, the war dance. They compared the day to those famous ones when the ocean had been churned, and the isle of Lanka sacked, as also to that other day when, in a great battle, the ocean-colored god had driven Arjuna's chariot. The *pinrerkkuravai*, the victory dance, was performed among the funeral pyres on the field of carnage.

With the crowned heads the demons built a huge fireplace. For cauldrons they used elephant skulls. Shoulder blades were their spoons. The demon-cooks gave a banquet to all the spirits of darkness. Drunk after their feast, they sang:

"Long live the king whose mighty and ever-righteous scepter has won a just battle."

Shenguttuvan of the ever-victorious spear had led his army in a glorious combat. Calling his messengers, he told them:

"Go and courteously assure of our favor all those in the northern country who honor our sacred books, and who, leading a sinless life, nourish the sacred fires with offerings."

The protecting king had won the battle and attained his goal. A few regiments, under the command of Villa-van-kôdai, were sent to wrench from the crown of the Himalaya the great stone in which the image of the goddess of Faithfulness was to be carved.

꙰ CANTO TWENTY-SEVEN ꙰

The Bathing of the Stone

Nîrppataikkâdai

The stele of stone was wrested from the proud Himalaya. It was given the shape of the Devoted Spouse who forced open the gateway of heaven. The statue was placed on the brilliantly crowned heads of Kanaka and Vijaya, to punish them for having dared fight Shenguttuvan, the king of the ferocious lance, who wears on his ankle the circlet of heroes. For eighteen *nâdis* [seven hours], he had taken the place of the cruel god of Death, devouring all the Aryan kings who had not acknowledged the supremacy of the proud southern Tamils. This battle was added to the three historic ones that had lasted respectively eighteen years, eighteen months, and eighteen days. *

With the aid of his troops, armed with victorious spears, Shenguttuvan had in a single day destroyed the countless armies of his assembled enemies. He returned to the bank of the Ganges, where the stone, already shaped to the likeness of the goddess of Faithfulness, was bathed, in accordance with sacred rules, by priests expert in the art of ritual. On the south bank of the river, where the waters are clear, the king settled in a vast camp built for him by the Aryan kings. There were magnificent arches, golden aisles, flower pavilions, apartments, vast gardens, lotus ponds, dance halls, all constructed with great art in honor of the suzerain king.

He sent for the sons of all the warriors who had died fighting the ambitious rulers of those vast lands, and had received husbands' wreaths from the nymphs of heaven. These soldiers had fought valiantly, never losing courage; they had lain, their heads severed, their spines broken, in pools of blood. They were but mercenaries, yet they had killed countless enemies before being hewn to pieces. They were still clinging to their swords as they fell dead, and in their stead the demons with sunken eyes danced the dance of victory and congratulated their ancestors. They had lain near their comrades, followed in death by faithful wives wearing all their jewels. As the vanguard of the army, they had placed victory flowers on their

---

* Respectively, the war of the gods and the demons, the war of Râma against Râvana, and the great Mahâbhârata war.

headgear before exterminating the forward units of the enemy troops. They had fallen near the mighty chariots, each with a painted staff for its pennon. Blood had dyed their bodies with its auspicious vermilion.

The king sent also for all the soldiers who had been heroes in the fight, who had severed the crowned heads of many an enemy whose courage could not be denied. The god of Death himself felt pity when he saw the wounded, with their broad chests ripped open through their armor. The triumph of the victorious king was sung by poets and bards. To each of them he gave an albizzia flower in gold, a present more precious than those distributed on the royal birthday. He adorned his own chest, as was his custom after a victory, with a wreath of palm leaves and aspera flowers.

While he was seated on his throne, Mâdalan the Brahmin entered. He said:

"Long live the king! A song on the seashore has brought a heavy burden to the crowned heads of Kanaka and Vijaya. Mighty king, conqueror of the sea-girt world, may you live forever!"

The king said:

"You speak in riddles, and the enemy kings may not grasp your purport. Explain the meaning of your words, Brahmin learned in the four *Vedas*!"

Mâdalan the Brahmin replied:

"A girl named Mâdhavi was quarreling with her lover on the seashore. Inspired by Fate, she sang some songs used as themes for her dance. Instead of mending their quarrel, the songs caused them to part. The lover returned to his wife and took her away to the ancient fortress-city of Madurai. There a leaf-garlanded king, who had committed a mistake, left the world after having killed this Kôvalan. The wife of the victim, O ruler of the Kudavar, came into your country. It is because of all this that her image is being transported today on the heads of northern monarchs.

"Kindly listen to the reasons that brought me here, king of kings, whose hand bears an illustrious spear. I had gone on a pilgrimage around Mount Podiyil, sacred abode of the great sage, and had bathed in the sacred waters of the Virgin's ocean. I was returning home when, inspired by Fate, I passed through Madurai, ruled by King Tennavan of the ever-sharp sword.

"When Mâdari heard that the beautiful girl left in her care had defeated the Pândya, with his immense army, just by an ankle bracelet, she came to the meeting-platform of the cowherds and spoke to the tribe there assembled: 'Cowherds! Kôvalan did no harm. The king committed a mistake, and I failed to protect a girl entrusted to my care. The royal parasol and the virtuous scepter have gone astray from the path of justice!' Having spoken, that night she threw herself into a bonfire and thus ended her life.

"At first the saintly Kavundi, well known for her virtues, was overcome by anger. When she heard of the death of the valorous king whose scepter had always stood for the rule of justice, she calmed herself and thought, 'Such is the fate of those who were my companions.' She resolved to fast unto death, and thus in a few days she ended her life on earth.

"I heard of these events and of the disaster that destroyed the glorious city of Madurai, ruled by a noble Pândya king who rode in a carriage of gold. Overwhelmed by sorrow, I returned to Puhâr, my native city, the Chôla's ancient capital. I informed all the notables

173

of these events. Kôvalan's father asked to be told the details of the whole tragedy that had overtaken his son and his daughter-in-law as well as the virtuous ruler of Madurai. Filled with despair, he distributed all his wealth, and entered the Sevenfold Monastery of Indra. There he leads an ascetic life with three hundred pious monks who spend all day in prayer, having renounced the world in the hope of escaping from the cycle of existence. His wife was unable to stand the news of her son's tragic death: broken by her sorrow, she died. Kannaki's father, too, gave away his riches and entered the order of the Ajîvakas, in which men of wisdom lead a life of fasting and penance. His noble spouse left the world a few days after his departure.

"When Mâdhavi heard of all these tragedies, she said to her kindly mother: 'As of today, I renounce all the pleasures of life. Do not allow Precious-Girdle to become a courtesan, for such a life leads to unhappiness.' She shaved off her garland-entwined hair, and entered a nunnery to study the teachings of Lord Buddha. It was I who had brought them the fatal news. That is why I have come to bathe in the waters of the sacred Ganges. Mighty king, may you live forever!"

The great Chêra monarch, who wears an ever-fresh garland of palm leaves, wild fig blossoms, and diospyros, then asked:

"May I know what happened to the wealthy country of the Pândya after its king had died?"

Mâdalan the Brahmin answered:

"Long live the ruler of the world! You once destroyed in a single day the nine parasols of nine great kings, your enemies, who had formed a league to dethrone your brother-in-law, Killivalavan, and refused to acknowledge his rights as legitimate heir to the kingdom. They had planned to destroy his prosperous country. You had to intervene and reset the wheel of destiny on its axle.

"O Poraiyan! You then wore a garland of palms to mark the success of the sword your right hand firmly holds. On another occasion, you uprooted the old margosa tree in whose branches the power of Palaiyan was hidden. Have patience to hear me.

"The victorious Vêr-Sheliyan, king of Korkai, sacrificed several thousand goldsmiths in a single day at the altar of the goddess of Faithfulness, who tore away her breast, and by whose curse ancient Madurai was put to shame and overwhelmed by the misfortunes that usually follow when a king fails in his duty. Another Pândya, also a descendant of the Moon's dynasty, took upon himself to protect the kingdom of the south. He was installed on the throne of Madurai. He is like a new Sun, risen in the glory of dawn on his one-wheeled car drawn by seven tall stallions whose harness bells ring joyfully. May you, great king who protects our country, live long and rule over the world for centuries to come, and may your name be immortal!"

While the king was carefully listening to the Brahmin, night was spreading over the land. When the sun had gone, a rich sunset reddened the western horizon. The crescent moon appeared among the stars. The wise monarch admired the splendor of the sunset. The court astrologer stood up and spoke the long-expected words: "Thirty-two months have passed since we left the city of Vanji. Long live the ruler of the world!" The king went alone through the camp, crossing the road of the chariots, lined with posts supporting canvas screens. He looked at the countless tents, small and large, resembling hills spread on the plain. Returning to his tent in the transversal avenue, he ascended again to his high throne, wrought from gold by palace craftsmen. Having sent for Mâdalan, he asked:

"Now that the old ruler of the fertile Chôla kingdom is dead, does the new king act with justice and with prudence?"

The Brahmin Mâdalan calmly answered:

"May you live forever, O king! How could the Chôla spear, that destroyed the three fortresses to the amazement of the gods adorned with sumptuous jewels, ever go astray from the path of righteousness? Could the scepter of a virtuous monarch, who cut off his own flesh to feed a starving kite and protect an innocent dove hopping on its tiny feet, now go astray from the path of duty? Even in times of great adversity, no fatal wrong can overcome the ruler of the land where the Kaveri flows."

At these words of the wise Brahmin, the great monarch who bears a lance and wears a wreath of palms, was pleased and said, "Brahmin Mâdalan, take this gift." And he gave him fifty *tulâms* of gold, a weight equal to his own.

He then allowed Nûrruvar Kannar and the Aryan kings to return to their prosperous countries. He ordered that a thousand emissaries known for the pride of the answers they gave to the haughty questions of enemy princes, be sent ahead to the Tamil country, taking with them the captured army chiefs who had attempted to escape from the battlefield in disguise. Each of these was bound to an Aryan *pêdi*, a male prostitute with drawn-in cheeks, black tufts, sunken dark eyes reddened at the corners, large earrings, red lips, white teeth, thin bamboo-like arms loaded with gold bracelets, fake breasts, thin waists, and circlets on their shapeless ankles, that made people laugh. One was chained to each of the prisoners, Kanaka and Vijaya, who had foolishly challenged the valor of the Tamil king, whose emblem is a garland of palm leaves.

At daybreak, after a quiet night, the bees in the vast lands watered by the Ganges began to hum, with the soft sound of harps, a song imploring the lotus to open its petals. Over the eastern hills the young sun appeared, lavishing his magnanimous gifts upon the lands. The victorious ruler of the western kingdom, adorning his neck with a garland of albizzia and northern diospyros, walked for the last time through his city of tents. Then, leading his victorious army, he set out for the south.

In the many-storied palace that rose into the sky, the goddess of Prosperity had made her permanent abode. The women's apartment was hung with rare gold tapestries, the work of able craftsmen, showing flowers festooned with pearls. Here and there, adroitly fastened by thin gold thread, were clear diamonds and sparkling gems. The gold bed of the queen showed exquisite workmanship. Its cushions had been filled with the feathers that the mating swan drops in the fields. The queen lay there restless, unable to find sleep in the absence of her beloved husband.

Maidservants had heard rumors of the great victory that the chariots and infantry led by Shenguttuvan had won on the field of battle. Expert in the art of imparting good news, they wished the queen long life, praised her, and said, "The melancholy days of solitude are over." The dwarfs and hunchbacks also came and said to her: "May beauty shine again! A great king has returned. Adorn your hair with flowers and perfume. Put on the ornaments suited to a great day."

Soon the songs of the hills, sung by the wild Kurava girls, could be heard:

"Short be the road of him who returns,
mounted on his racing elephant,
wearing the wreath of albizzia
and northern diospyros."

Seated on the hillside slopes, the girls laughed as they greeted the forest guards. Drunk on the honey taken from the hives bees build in the bamboo forest, they forgot to throw stones at the wild elephants leaving the dark jungle to rest in the millet fields.

The rough peasants, too, could be heard singing as they ploughed their fields:

"Then after he had razed the fortresses
of northern kings, the Kudavar ruler
sent donkeys to plough up the ground
where the proud towns of enemies had stood,
and sowed white millet on their sites.
And now he has returned. O my bullocks,
you shall be freed from yokes today.
It is the birthday of the king,
and every prisoner will be unchained."

On the steps leading down to the river An-Porunai, soap paste, scented powders, and the flower garlands of the bathers spread their colors like a rainbow. From there could be heard the clear sounds of the shepherds' flutes and voices raised in song:

"The archer has returned,
bringing a herd, well fed,
from the famed Himalaya.
Dear little sheep, you
shall play with these foreigners."

In their tufts of hair the shepherds tied charming garlands of lotuses, dear to the bees, and sweet-scented water lilies. After bringing the royal flocks to drink at the river, they stood on the pandanus stalks.

From farther away, the lusty songs of the sailors could be heard:

"King Vânavan has come back to tickle
the shoulders and the shapely nipples
of his young queen. O lovely girls!
Now we can sing him the heroes' song.
To get the reward of his victory,
he will give up his wreath of flowers."

The daughters of the fishermen sang love songs on the beach, seated under the shade of *punnai* trees, on sand brought in by the foaming waves. They played with balls, and with hands loaded with bangles they stole lustrous pearls from gaping oyster shells.

Listening to these songs with strange emotion, the all-powerful queen once more slipped over her wrists her well-fitting bracelets. Seated on a swift elephant, Shenguttuvan, wearing his most stately crown, with an albizzia garland round his neck, entered Vanji. The citizens welcomed him with a procession of chariots drawn by elephants.

⚶ CANTO TWENTY-EIGHT ⚶

The Consecration

Nadukarkâdai

Evening, which incites flowers to open and inspires men to pray, took possession of the ancient town of Vanji, famous for the conquests of its monarchs, for their victorious sword and proud golden parasol, like the full moon, that covers the earth with its shade.

Young girls with shining gold bangles placed offerings of fresh flowers before the bright glow of the lamps they had lit. They prayed: "May the gods bless the ruler of the universe." Women, their eyes darkened with collyrium, their young breasts firm and round, passionately embraced the warriors whose swords had led them to victory and who were now returned from their adventure wearing palm garlands, gold chains, and flower wreaths. Some had had their chests pierced through by the sharp tusks of furious elephants, some showed deep scars made by a sword's sharp edge, some had had their lustrous breasts struck by painful arrows, and some had had their broad shoulders, now adorned with wreaths, split by lances.

Toward these men the women cast burning glances resembling the flowery arrows shot by the god Kâma, whose pennant bears a fish. These arrows were sped by the bows of dark lashes, set in faces like the moon shining among clouds of lustrous hair fragrant with incense and perfume. These arrows brought the love messages of tender hearts to the warriors, loaded with chains of gold. The soldiers cheered the twilight, which they called the soothing balm of lonely hearts. The girls' bodies seemed as soft as new mango shoots. Smiles of pleasure appeared on their red lips; their long, carp-shaped eyes slitted as if to touch their ears. Their bodies were a feast for the lewd gaze of thirsty warriors so long deprived of love's sweet games.

The evening brought the soldiers new prospects of pleasure: women with youthful faces who wore the dot of musk on their foreheads. Their curly hair, their flower wreaths round which the bees clustered, were thrown into disorder during the love-play. Looking into small mirrors, they straightened their garments. With perfect grace, each took from its case a harp ornamented with subtle art. On the strings fastened to its precious neck each began by playing the basic scale in which C is taken as tonic. Then they played in the *kurinji* mode in which the second note is taken as the drone.

Evening vanished, abandoning the world to the gentle rule of the moon, which, as it rose, received the homage of the earth. To the people of glorious Vanji, the moon recalled the face of King Shenguttuvan, as he appears in the great audience hall, his ankles brushed by the hair of the defeated kings.

All lovers and their mistresses enrolled in the army of the young god of Lust, the great archer whose arrows are made of flowers. The god of Lust established himself as the supreme ruler of all the terraces that the moon bathed in its cooling light. He triumphed also in shadowy groves, carpeted with fallen petals, in dance pavilions where fine sand had been spread, under dark fragrant bowers, on soft beds, on cool verandas. The gentle moon drew over all lovers her silvery mantle of cooling light. Round the center of the ancient city stood high ramparts decked with flags. The audience hall of the golden palace rose as massive and splendid as Mount Meru, the great polar mountain, surrounded on all sides by the ocean.

Vênmâl, the virtuous queen, came to look at the moon. She was followed by maids wearing brilliant bracelets, who carried lamps. There were also girl musicians, playing drums tuned with clay paste and harps shaped like bows, and singing tender and moving melodies. Then came dwarfs and hunchbacks, bringing musk and white sandal paste. Eunuchs, dressed like women, carried incense sticks and perfumes. Young girls brought mats strewn with flowers, while servants carried the mirrors women constantly need, as well as fresh garments and brightly painted jars. It was to an exquisitely furnished roof that the king, lord of the sea-encircled world, ascended with his queen.

To amuse the king, a Brahmin boy dancer from Puraiyûr, famed for the art of its priests learned in the four *Vedas*, performed the dance of the hermaphrodite which the god Shiva once danced after uniting with Umâ in a single body. The circlet at his right ankle rang, a small drum resounded in his swiftly moving hand, his reddened right eye expressed changing moods, his tuft of matted hair shook briskly when he moved; yet all the while the anklet bells on his left foot remained silent, the bracelets at his wrist showed no movement, his belt did not vibrate, his breast did not quiver, the jewels did not swing on the feminine half of his person. His carefully set hair did not uncurl.

When the dancer had sung the praise of the world's supreme sovereign, a secretary informed the king of the arrival of Mâdalan the good Brahmin, together with Nîlan. The king entered the audience hall and sent for them, together with the other officeholders. After paying his respects to the king through the officers of the throne, Nîlan told him:

"King who wears the garland of diospyros and the anklet of victory! We went, with the captive kings, to the city of the Chôla Shembiyan, and sent him our respects through his palace officers. Seated in the splendid audience hall built for him by the kings of Vajra, Avanti, and far Magadha, he made an improper remark to the commander of the chariot corps, the first of the army: 'I can hardly see the merit of capturing on a battlefield those who, having shown their courage, then abandoned their parasols and swords to hide in civilian clothes.'

"We soon took leave of the magnanimous Chôla on whose breast gleam magnificent jewels. We then went to Madurai, the famous capital of the Pândya, whose spear is powerful. He told us: 'We fail to see the meaning of a victory in which kings who gave up the fight to don monastic robes are the victims of anger and hatred. It also seems improper that Shenguttuvan should have taken the staff of the white parasol that the Aryan kings place on the necks of their tall elephants, to turn it into a phallic emblem of Jayanta, son of Indra, while he himself had gone to worship Shiva and his consort Umâ at Kuyilâluvam in the Himalaya.'"

While Nîlan was reporting the disparaging words of the two kings, Shenguttuvan laughed at first; but soon his eyes were casting flames. Mâdalan, his wise counselor, stood up and said:

"King of kings! Your renown is immortal, and we hope you may live for many years to come. When you destroyed the mighty kingdom of Viyalûr, famed for its lotus ponds and for its elephants that roam on the mountains where pepper grows in abundance, you won a famous victory on the field of Nêrivâyil over nine kings who wore garlands of wild fig leaves. Leaving your army of heavy horse-chariots in camp near Idumbil, you fought for many days upon the sea, following your enemy to a great distance. Later you defeated the Aryan kings advancing to the banks of the furious Ganges.

"King! Today you wear a victor's garlands and you possess a mighty army. You are like a lion among men, and already you know all the things a great man need learn. Give up anger! And may the days of your life be as many as the grains of sand in the bed of the cool and famous river An-Porunai.

"King of the sea-encircled world, may you live many years! Pray hearken to my words. Fifty years have already passed since you undertook the charge of protecting the land, yet you have not offered up any great sacrifice to please the gods; you have only contributed to the hecatombs of war. Sword in hand, you have accomplished all you desired.

"One king of this city already won fame for destroying the Kadambu country beyond the sea. Another showed his prowess by carving his emblem, the bow, on the Himalaya. Still another, as reward for a few poems, enabled the Brahmin Pâlai Gautamanâr, well versed in the *Vedas,* to obtain a place in heaven. Yet another compelled death's messengers to overtake their prey only in the order that he would allow. And it was a Chêra who penetrated the hills where the rich kingdom of the barbarian Greeks lay hidden.

"Still another Chêra, after having chased his enemy and his army far from the battlefield, had the strength to capture him in the town he had fortified. One more king of your illustrious clan bathed in the river Ayirai whose water mixes with that of both oceans. Another bade the genie Chatushka come to Vanji and offered him a sacrifice of wine.

"Yet none of these great men was able to escape death. You know that this body cannot last forever. You were able to see, in your battle with the Aryan kings who had insulted the courageous Tamils, that Fortune cannot be trusted by any man who lives on generous Earth.

"Just king! There is no need to remind you that youth cannot be eternal. Protecting king! The hairs upon your chest where the goddess of Fortune rests have now become pure silver. We know that sometimes divine souls become incarnated in men's bodies, and that the souls that leave dumb animals may be reborn in the pitiful bodies of demons. Man is but an actor. He cannot always play the same role. It is not false to say that our life after death will be determined by our actions in our present life. King, whose chest is adorned with a necklace wrought of seven crowns, may the wheel of power add ever more noble actions to the list of honors of your illustrious family!

"Wielder of a mighty sword! If I dare speak before you as I am doing now, it is not to obtain a rich present. It is because I cannot bear to see a fine soul in a fine body being dragged down toward the low paths of common behavior. King! You have reached the limits of knowledge. Your aim now should be to perform sacrifices, with the aid of good priests learned in the four *Vedas*. Thus you would please the gods.

"You may always postpone a good deed till tomorrow, but your soul, gradually fashioned by the study of the scripture, may abandon your body at any time. In the whole sea-girt world no one can say for how long he will live. May you and your queen remain with us for many years, flattered by kings who wear the ring of submission and bow at your feet. May our good king live long, protecting our lovely land century after century."

The tongue of the Brahmin, learned in the four *Vedas*, ploughed the king's mind and sowed its wisdom there. Soon these seeds bore fruit. Desirous of gathering a richer harvest of merits, the king, who wears ringing circlets on his ankles, called priests expert in the ritual of sacrifice, who had learned their art from teachers well versed in the traditional explanation of the *Vedas*. He ordered them to prepare a great sacrifice, following all the instructions of Mâdalan.

He then ordered that the prisons, where the Aryan kings had been held, should be thrown open; he had them removed from Vanji, that ancient and glorious city, to the home of Vêlâvikkô, surrounded by lakes and gardens. He promised these kings that they might return to the land of their birth on the day after the end of the great sacrifice. He was happy to say in their presence: "Friend Villavan-kôdai, take care of their comfort. Treat them as befits great princes." Orders were sent to Alambilvêl and Ayakkanakkar that the prisons be opened and cleaned, and that taxes be refunded to all citizens.

The Chôla king, who wears a garland of fig leaves, pointed out the noble path of duty. The Faithful Wife, whom the whole world now worships, had proved the truth of the Tamil proverb that says, "The virtue of women is of no use where the king has failed first to establish the reign of justice." Kannaki had compelled the Pândya, protector of the southern country, to recognize that a king can no longer live when his scepter has gone astray from the path of duty. The Chêra, king of the western lands, had shown that his anger could never be appeased until the weight of his vow had crushed the northern kings. The anger of the Faithful Wife, transformed into a flame born of her breast, had destroyed ancient Madurai. This unhappiest of women then entered our country, where she was seen under the shade of a golden kino. In honor of this great woman, wise Brahmins, priests, astrologers, and artisans built, according to the prescribed rules, a temple whose design was approved by all architects. In this temple there can be seen today the image of the Faithful Wife, carved with great art, after worship of the god Shiva who dwells on the highest peaks of mountains, in the great stone brought from the

Himalaya, where the gods have their abode. The image is adorned with priceless ornaments, models of perfect craftsmanship. It is worshiped with daily offerings. At the entrance to the temple stand the images of the rulers of the four directions in space. The lion among men who had established his sway over the northern countries came in person to perform the rites of the consecration of the image. He left orders that every day the goddess be worshiped and oblations be offered at her altar.

✣ CANTO TWENTY-NINE ✣

The Benediction

Vâlttukkâdai

INTRODUCTION

Shenguttuvan of Vanji once defeated the Kongu in a legendary battle, and then advanced to the famous Ganges. He was the son of King Chêralâtan who had ruled from the south cape to the Himalaya. His mother, a daughter of the Chôla, belonged to the illustrious descendants of the Sun. Shenguttuvan was a man of quarrelsome temper. Some holy men, returning from the land beyond the Ganges, told him that certain northern kings, assembled on the occasion of a princess's marriage, had exchanged impudent remarks about the Tamil kings, who had already defeated them once, when they went to carve their three emblems—the bow, the fish, and the tiger—on the brow of the Himalaya. The Aryan kings boasted: "No head that wears a crown can vie with ours."

The decision to bring down a great stone from the

Himalaya was like the stick that starts a hoop. It led Shenguttuvan to do battle against the kings of the Aryan country. After the great success of his expedition, he remained for some time near the Ganges, receiving all the honors due to a visiting emperor. He had insisted that a great stone should be brought from the Himalaya on the heads of the Aryan kings, and that it should be bathed, according to custom, in the sacred waters of the Ganges. His anger quenched, he returned to Vanji. There, with great magnificence, he consecrated a new temple in which there stands a tall image of Kannaki, whose youthful breast, torn away in her wrath, had been the source of all these great events. There the kings of the world worship her and bring her their offerings.

Shortly after, Mâshâttuvân chose to become a monk. He had heard the noble Brahmin depict the terrible ordeal of Kannaki, whose moonlike face was drenched with tears that flowed incessantly from her dark, carp-shaped eyes. With hair unbound and soiled with dust, she entered the palace and cursed the king—responsible for the protection of justice—for the great injustice meted out to Kôvalan, for his death at the hand of a vile soldier. She stood before his throne until the king fell dead, destroyed by his unjust action. And his wife followed him in death.

On hearing the news, the nurse and foster sister of Kannaki, as well as Devandi, who had taken refuge with the divine Shâttan, went together to the city of Madurai, hoping to bring Kannaki back. There, they learned of the disaster her breast had caused. They visited Aiyai, the cowgirl daughter of old Mâdari, who had died after the departure of the woman who had been entrusted to her care. All together, they followed the road that runs along the bank of the Vaigai. Climbing the mountain, they came to the palace of King Shenguttuvan, who had built a temple to the goddess of Faithfulness. They explained their various connections with Kannaki.

DEVANDI'S SPEECH

You see in me the friend of the woman that three crowned heads worship. I am the companion of the goddess brought from the north and bathed in the sacred Ganges. I was the comrade of her whose wrists are covered with precious bracelets. Recognize me as the true friend of the goddess of the Chôla country.

THE NURSE'S SPEECH

You see in me the nurse of the long-eyed lady who never showed anger toward the beautiful and lowly born Mâdhavi, and who did not fear to enter the dangerous forest in which all the wells had gone dry. Recognize me as the foster mother of the goddess of ever-cool Puhâr.

THE FOSTER SISTER'S SPEECH

You see in me the companion of the lady with gold ornaments who, faithfully following her dear husband, went away without a word to the woman who had given her birth, or to the nurse who had brought her up, or even to her friend. She knew but one duty, that of a wife. Recognize me as the friend of the lady of Pûmpuhâr.

THE LAMENTATION OF DEVANDI

before the image of Kannaki

My penance has borne no fruit, for I did not understand the meaning of your dream when you related it to me.

What a fearful error was mine! Woman with the thick, braided hair! The day your mother heard the story of the disaster your torn-off breast had caused, she died, unable to bear her sorrow. Can you hear me, dear friend? Your good mother-in-law died too. Can you hear, friend?

THE LAMENTATION OF THE NURSE

Mâshâttuvân heard the story of the deathblow that an unworthy man gave Kôvalan, and the story of the end of the Pândya king. Losing all taste for life, he distributed his vast fortune and entered a monastery. Did you hear all this, O Mother? Did you also hear the story of how Mânâikan renounced the world, O Mother?

THE LAMENTATION OF THE FOSTER SISTER

Mâdhavi heard the news of her lover's terrible death. She listened to the long story of your own sufferings. She overheard people in the street speaking of her with disgust and contempt. She lost courage. Often she went to the sermons preached by the monks under the *bodhi* tree. She gave all her wealth to the poor and became a nun. O my companion, can you hear? And friend, have you heard also that Precious-Girdle too renounced the world?

THE LAMENTATION OF DEVANDI

showing Aiyai

This girl is the daughter of the woman who gave up her life in despair, who said: "I shall destroy my body by fire, for I failed to protect the girl who had taken shelter under my roof and who was entrusted to my care by the saint." Can you see, friend, this Aiyai with her lovely white teeth? Can you see, friend, your handsome niece?

Shenguttuvan spoke:
"I have seen ... What is it ... ? Am I dreaming ... ?
Ah ... ! In the sky, a marvelous vision ... ! A woman,
slender as a lightning-flash ... ! Gold circlets gleam at
her ankles. She wears a girdle, bangles at her wrists, sparkling diamonds in her ears, and splendid ornaments of
finest gold."

Kannaki, goddess of Faithfulness, told Shenguttuvan:
"Those terrible events were not the fault of the
Pândya king. He is today the honored guest of the ruler of
heaven. And I am treated as his daughter. I go to play on
the mountain where Venvêlân lives. My friends, will
you join me?"

One of the Vanji girls sang:
"Girls of Vanji! Slender-waisted girls, like Vanji's
lianas. Girls with lacquer-reddened feet, living in the
palace of a victorious king! Join your voices to mine!
Come, sing! Praise the girl whose breast reduced Madurai
to ashes and whose ankle bracelet destroyed a king. Let
us sing the praise of the daughter of Tennavan. She came
to our country, and our king revered her. He said: 'A
Pândya cannot live when the rod of justice has been bent
in his hand.' Let us praise this beautiful girl. Come and
sing hymns to the Pândya's daughter."

THE GIRLS' CHORUS

The gods have called her daughter of a king.
She's lithe as a liana; people say
she is the daughter of the Vaigai.
We sing the praise of Vânavan,
great-hearted Vânavan, the Chêra king.
The gods themselves shall sing the praise
of him, the ruler of the Vaigai.

Blessed be the king who abandoned life at the sight of the tears of a woman to whom merciless fate had brought misfortune.

Blessed be the ancient dynasty that rules Madurai, the ancient city girt by the plentiful waters of the Vaigai. Blessed be the Pândya king.

Blessed be the king who could compel the tall fair monarchs, rulers over the kingdoms of the north, to carry on their heads, made higher still by crowns, the statue he had wrested from the king of mountains.

Blessed be the king who owns the happy land where the river Kâverî flows. Let us, all together, sing the glory of Puhâr, girls whose tresses are entwined with flowers.

SONG OF THE WOODEN BALL

Ammânai

Will you tell me, wooden ball,
who he was, that mighty man
who governed the entire world
encircled by the sea,
and once kept watch before
the king of heaven's fort?
Do you know, hard wooden ball,
that he, the guard before those gates,
was the famous Chôla king
who brought down the three cities
that were flying in the sky?

Wooden ball, we sing in praise
of Puhâr, the great capital
of the Chôla conqueror,

whom even heaven honors—
he who sat in scales to give
a full pound of his flesh
to save a poor dove's life.
This was the king, O wooden ball,
from whom a cow asked justice.

We sing the charming city
of Puhâr, the capital
where great kings rule, O wooden ball—
they who carved a tiger head
upon the Himalaya's face.
The elephants that give support
to the corners of the sky
observed his feat, and did not blink.
O wooden ball, the king who carved
a tiger on the northern peaks
was the same conqueror who spread
the shade of his great parasol
over the whole world.

Wooden ball, we sing the praise
of the beautiful Puhâr,
capital of famous kings.
Wooden ball, why do young girls,
putting on their jewelry,
sing songs in their homes,
while they hold hard wooden balls?

The purpose is, O wooden ball,
to obtain from the mighty king
who wears a wreath of flowers
a kiss on their alluring,
well-rounded, nascent breasts.
And while the king bestows a kiss
upon these tempting youthful breasts,

we shall sing a little song
unto the glory of Puhâr,
city of love, O wooden ball.

Kanduka

Girl, flexible as a liana,
your gold necklace tinkles in harmony
with the light girdles that confine our waists
slender as lightning-bolts.
Run! Strike the bouncing ball!
Cheer: Long live the Pândya! Long may he live!

We shall strike the bouncing ball,
and we shall sing, we shall sing:
Long life to him who wears on his broad chest
the necklace of the king of gods.
Come! Go! Sit! Dance!
—front, back, and everywhere,
as if a brilliant lightning-bolt
were falling from Heaven to Earth.

We shall strike the bouncing ball,
and we shall sing, we shall sing:
Long life to him who wears on his broad chest
the necklace of the king of gods.
The bouncing ball does not stay in the hand,
it does not fly to Heaven, it does not leave the Earth.
Come, strike the ball and sing!
Cheer: Long live the Pândya! Long may he live!

Strike the bouncing ball and sing:
Long life to him who wears on his broad chest
the necklace of the king of gods.

SONG OF THE SWING

Sit on the painted swing, hung from thick ropes.
Standing near Aiyai we shall push, with outspread hands.
We beat the time, and sing the praise
of that great king who conquered Kadambu.
Let's swing the swing and roll our eyes
like swaying palm-tree leaves.
Let's swing the swing and sing
the bow carved on the mountain peak.
We'll praise the courage, valor, glory
of Poraiyan, the monarch of the hills,
the noble Chêra who provided such
abundant rations to his soldiers in the war
of the five against the hundred.

Let's swing the swing, our hair
floating like clouds around us.
We shall sing, as we swing,
how Kadambu was overthrown.
Let's sing the praises of our king,
the ruler who protects the world
up to its end, the Virgin's Cape.
His standard bears three emblems,
the bow, the tiger, and the fish;
his might spreads even to the fertile land
of the crude Greeks, who speak a barbarous tongue.

Let's swing the swing, bending our waists
frail as a lightning-bolt; let's sing
the prowess of the king who carved
the bow, his emblem, on the peaks.

SONG OF THE PESTLE

The girls of Puhâr gather under the shade of the portias
in bloom to crush rare pearls, using sugar-cane sticks as

pestles. They sing the praise of Shembiyan's car, and they worship the wheel, the emblem of his power. They praise his broad shoulders loaded with flower wreaths. They know no other song. Truly, this is the only song the girls of Puhâr know how to sing.

The girls of Madurai, that city of the high towers, crush pearls with coral pestles celebrated by poets. They sing the praise of Panchavan, whose emblem is the fish, and who wears on his broad shoulders the beautiful necklace of the king of heaven. They know no other song. Truly, their only song tells of a wreath of margosa and a Pândya monarch.

The girls of Vanji crush their priceless pearls in mortars of sandalwood, with pestles made of ivory. They sing the praise of the Chêra who wears the wreath of victory since he defeated Kadambu beyond the sea. They know no other song. Truly, their only song is that which depicts a wreath of heart-gladdening palm leaves.

Those who fail to worship the sacred feet of Poraiyan, whose bow is tall, miss their chance to bless the sovereign of the world. Kannaki, famous daughter of a monarch, blessed him: "Long live Shenguttuvan."

✻✻ CANTO THIRTY ✻✻

The Consequences

Varantarukâdai

The great king who conquered the countries of the north had a vision of Kannaki in her celestial form. He looked at Devandi and asked:

"Who is Precious-Girdle, of whom you spoke with affection? Why did she renounce the world? Please tell me her story."

Devandi blessed the king, then said:

"May your glory always increase and your kingdom be ever prosperous!" She told him how Precious-Girdle, already renowned among the dancers, whose hips are always decked with ornaments, had renounced the pleasures of the world. She depicted her abundant black hair, parted into five plaits, and her cool eyes with their corners charmingly reddened. She spoke of her innocent grace. "Her pearl-like teeth, sheltered behind her tender coral lips, were not yet fully grown, her breasts had just begun to rise, her hips were taking shape, her waist was growing slender, and her charming sex had started to blossom. Her thighs were rounding out; her tender feet could hardly bear the weight of her anklets; her skin was like satin. Yet the young men of noble families did not treat her as they treat dancing girls, and no dance master had taught her his art.

"The good mother of Mâdhavi asked her: 'Tell me your intentions!' 'What should I do?' Mâdhavi called Precious-Girdle: 'Come, dear modest girl!' She cut off her tresses still entwined with flowers. Enraged, the god of Love threw away his sugar-cane bow and his flowery arrows. Precious-Girdle then entered a convent and accepted the severe Buddhist rule.

"When the king and the citizens of the town heard this news, they were as sad as if a priceless jewel had been dropped into the sea before their very eyes. The saintly man who accepted her into the fold said gently: 'The charming girl has expressed her wish to leave the world. I lamented at the sight of this lovely girl deprived so young of her beauty.'"

After she had answered the king's question, Devandi seemed to enter into a trance. The flowers in her hair fell to the ground; her contracted eyebrows began to throb; her lips, drawn against her white teeth, showed a strange contraction. Her voice changed, and her face became covered with pearls of sweat. Her large eyes grew red. She flung her arms about in threatening gestures. Suddenly her legs moved; she stood upright. No one could recognize her. She seemed in a state of stupor. Her dry tongue uttered inspired words before the king and Mâdalan, his learned counselor.

"In the group of women, good, beautiful, and shy, who came here for the installation of the image of the goddess, are two twin girls, born of the lovely wife of Arattan Shetti. Here also is the granddaughter of the priest Shêdak-Kudumbi, employed in the service of the golden temple where the Lord of the Universe sleeps, resting on the coils of a divine serpent. Near the temple of Mangala-devî, the goddess of Luck, there is a hill that rises to the sky. On its red summit there is a rock surrounded by marshes. From it spring several streams whose beds are composed of white stones, resembling rice but small as mustard seeds, mixed with pebbles red as coral-tree flowers.

"Those who bathe in these streams recall all the events of their past existence. I went there, filled a pitcher with the water, and left it with you, good Brahmin Mâdalan, while you sat near a temple door, asking you to take great care of it. This is the pitcher you are carrying today in your net bag. This water shall never lose its power till the day the sun and moon shall vanish. If you sprinkle it over the three girls, they will remember their past lives. I am Shâttan, the Magician, speaking through the body of a Brahmin woman."

Shenguttuvan was stunned by amazement. He turned to Mâdalan, who told him joyfully:

"King! We are now reaching the end of this great adventure. A young woman, Mâlati, once gave some milk to the son of her husband's second wife. Fate turned against her: the child died. In her despair she prayed to the Magician, who, to help her, took the form of the child. He said, 'Mother, give up all fear!' And he took away her sorrow. After this miracle, Shâttan the Magician grew up as that child under the care of a tender mother and the co-wife, in the well-known family of the Kâppiya. He married Devandi, going with her round the sacred fire. After living with her eight years, he revealed himself to her in his celestial form of eternal adolescence. Then he disappeared, telling her, 'Come to see me in my temple.'

"When I went to visit the shrine of the goddess of Luck, the Magician, taking the form of a Brahmin, appeared beside me and left under my care his net bag with a water jar. Today this great sage has appeared again before our eyes, and, through the mouth of a Brahmin woman, he orders me to use the water of the jar. King! Shall we sprinkle it over the girls, and thus learn what this is all about?"

After the aspersion, the children recovered the memory of their past existence. One of them began to lament:

"My daughter! My only comfort! Without saying a word to me, who had shown you my sympathy in your hour of trouble, when your husband had left you and was misbehaving, you went to a foreign city in the sole company of your lord and there you disappeared in an ocean of suffering. Dear child, will you never come back again to share my worries?"

The second girl also began to wail:

"You left during the night, taking away my dear daughter-in-law who had long lived with me. I became like a madwoman after your departure. I can bear my pain no longer. Shall you never come back, dear son?"

"I had gone to bathe in the waters of the Vaigai in spate. When I returned, I heard the news from some boys in the town. I did not find you in my hut. O dear, dear child, where did you hide?"

The little girls, with bangles on their wrists, cried and lamented with their lisping lips. Tears filled their eyes; they talked as grown-up people do, to the astonishment of the victorious king whose chest was covered with gold ornaments. The king, who wore the garland of palm leaves and the victor's anklet, raised his eyes toward Mâdalan, who wore a sacred thread across his chest. The priest blessed him and said:

"King among kings! May your days be countless!" He related what he had remembered. "The three women were attached to Kannaki in their previous lives. Kôvalan obtained a place in Paradise because he had once saved a Brahmin's life by seizing the tusks of a mad elephant. But these women had no meritorious deed to their credit, so they could not follow Kannaki to her new heavenly abode. Because of their deep attachment to that lianalike woman, who had fearlessly come to the town of Vanji, these two mothers have been reborn as two twin girls, to the great joy of the simple and modest wife of Arattan Shetti. As for the old cowherd woman, who became so attached to the charming young bride and danced for her the dance of Love, she is today the granddaughter of a priest of Vishnu, named Shêdak-Kudumbi.

"Is it not strange to observe that those who have performed pious works can enter the heavens, while those whose attachments are to the things of this earth are born again? Good and evil actions must bear their fruits. All that is born must die, and all that dies must be reborn. These simple truths are nothing new.

"Since your birth you have been under the protection of him who rides a divine bull, and you have built your own reputation among the monarchs of the world. You have seen, as clearly as an object held in your hand, the results of actions and the forms of heavenly saints. May you protect the land for many years to come. May your days be countless, gracious king!"

Pleased with the words of Mâdalan, the king presented sumptuous gifts to the temple of the goddess of Faithfulness who had torn off her breast and engendered the flames that destroyed the resounding capital of the celebrated Pândya whom all poets have sung. He ordered that there be worship every day in the shrine, and that Devandi be responsible for offerings of flowers, incense, and perfume.

The world's king walked three times around the sanctuary, and bowed before the image. He was followed by the Aryan kings, freed from prison, and many other ruling monarchs, such as the prince of the Kongus, the king of Mâlva, the king of Kudagu, and even Gajabâhu, the king of Ceylon. They had come to worship the goddess and to ask her blessings:

"Manifest your divine presence in our country, as you did on the auspicious day of Imayavaranban's sacrifice!"

A clear voice was heard from the sky, saying:

"All your requests are granted."

Shenguttuvan, the other kings, and soldiers of his valorous armies sang hymns to the goddess with as much enthusiasm as if she had granted to them to be freed from the cycle of their lives.

Accompanied by Mâdalan, the Brahmin speaker of the truth, and by kings loaded with anklets that made a constant din when they bowed before him, Shenguttuvan entered the sacrificial hall. I* followed him. Devandi, possessed by a god, approached me. She said:

"In the rich audience hall of ancient Vanji, you once sat beside your father. You frowned when the astrologer suddenly predicted that you would inherit the throne. This caused a shock to your brother, Shenguttuvan, famous leader of the army's chariots, who wore a wreath of fragrant red cottonwood flowers. You wanted to become a monk, and you entered the monastery of Gunavâyirkôttam. Standing with great humility before the chapter of the monks, you formally renounced the burdens of this world, to gain a crown of happiness beyond the conception of the human mind."

[I, Ilangô Adigal, replied:]

"Wise and virtuous people! You have already heard the words of good will spoken by this child of the gods, who, in her kindness, agreed to tell us her story. You should now raise your thoughts above pleasure and pain. Here are some of the rules of behavior meant for all the inhabitants of the vast and prosperous land:

Seek God and serve those who are near Him.
Do not tell lies.
Avoid slander.
Avoid eating the flesh of animals.
Do not cause pain to any living thing.
Be charitable, and observe fast days.
Never forget the good others have done to you.

---

* Here finally the author, Ilangô Adigal, speaks himself in the first person.

Avoid bad company.
Never give false evidence.
Do not disguise the truth.
Stay near those who fear God.
Avoid the company of atheists.
Do not associate with other men's wives.
Care for the sick and the dying.
Uphold domestic virtues.
Get rid of your bad habits.
From this day on, abstain from drink, theft, sensuality,
   falsehood, bad company.
Youth fades, wealth vanishes, this body is only a
   temporary dwelling.
The days of your life are numbered.
You cannot escape from your fate.
Seek the help of everything that leads you to the
   ultimate goal of life.

CONCLUSION OF THE CHAPTER

Among the three monarchs, the western king, born in the immortal Chêra line, wore the garland of suzerainty. The Book of Vanji has related the great deeds of his reign, his virtue, his courage, his rare accomplishments. We have described his ancient and wealthy capital with its festivities, the apparitions of the gods, the prosperity of the realm, the fertility of the land, the abundance of stocks, the music, dances, and theatre, the army and its fierce sword-wielding warriors who won all their battles so decisively, their victories against an enemy who had to be pursued far on the raging sea, and the expedition to the Ganges.

Thus ends *The Lay of the Ankle Bracelet*. It contains in brief the story of Precious-Girdle [theme of another novel, the *Mani-mêkalai*]. Like a mirror reflecting the mountains, this story reflects the cool Tamil land that extends from the Virgin's Cape to the Venkata Hills, and is bound both to east and west by the sea. This land is divided into several countries. In some, people speak pure Tamil; in others, various dialects. In its five main regions men and gods dwell, seeking to fulfill the three aims of life: virtue, wealth, and pleasure.

In clear and restrained language made into faultless verse, this story pictures *aham*, love, and *puram*, war. It contains songs, and describes stringed instruments, music and musicians, the theatre and its rules, the various forms of dance, and lays down the classical rules for pure dance, the love-dance, and character dances.

Appendices

APPENDIX I

PREAMBLE*

Kuravas from the hills gathered near the Kunnavayil temple, dwelling place of the venerable prince who was the brother of Kudakkôcchêral Ilangô, Chêra king of the west. This prince had preferred a hermit's life to the throne. They reported to him the following events:

"A woman who had lost one breast was seen under a kino tree covered with gold flowers. Suddenly the king of heaven arrived, followed by the woman's husband. Before our eyes they rose together into the sky. We came here to inform Your Grace of these remarkable events."

Shâttan, the great Tamil poet, was with the prince. He said:

"I can explain this miracle." He then related the following story. "In the ancient town of Puhâr, immortal capital of the Chôla kings who wear the wreath of fig leaves, there lived a rich merchant named Kôvalan. He dissipated his great wealth in the pleasures offered him

* This Preamble is considered by the ancient commentators not to belong to the original text, whose contents it summarizes. We therefore give it only in an appendix.

by a dancing girl expert in her art. He had a wife named Kannaki. With her he went to Madurai, the capital of the celebrated Pândya kingdom. In need of funds, he wished to sell her beautiful ankle bracelet, and went into the main bazaar looking for a buyer. There he showed the ankle bracelet to a goldsmith, who said, 'Only a queen can wear such jewelry.' He suggested that Kôvalan wait near his shop, and ran to the palace to inform the king that he had found the thief of the queen's gold anklet. At that moment Kôvalan's hour of destiny had come. The king, who wears a wreath of margosa, did not bother to make an investigation, but simply ordered a guard to put the thief to death and bring back the queen's bracelet. The wife of Kôvalan found herself abandoned and shed abundant tears. She tore away one of her breasts, adorned by a string of pearls. By the power of her virtue, she burned down the great city of Madurai and called down upon the Pândya kings the anger of the gods. This is the woman, of great fame and rare virtue, of whom the hillmen have spoken."

Hearing these words, Prince Ilangô asked:

"Can you tell us in what mysterious way fate acts, as you claim it does?"

Shâttan replied:

"Listen, pious man! Once, in the town of Madurai, I was taking my rest at midnight under the silver porch of a temple called Manrappodiyil, consecrated to Lord Shiva, the god who wears a laburnum flower on his brow. I suddenly saw a genie, one of the guardians of the city, and before him stood the Devoted Wife, who seemed in great distress. The genie said to her: 'Woman, fearful flames spring from your breast! The time has come for actions performed in past lives to bear their fruit. In a previous life, the wife of a merchant coming from Singapore, the immortal city, cursed you and your husband. Lovely creature with flowing hair! After fourteen days you shall again meet the man you love, no longer in his earthly appearance but in his celestial form!'

"I heard these simple words, and thought that a poem should be written to illustrate three eternal precepts:

1. *Divine Law* (Dharma) *takes the form of death when a king goes astray from the path of duty.*
2. *All must bow before a chaste and faithful wife.*
3. *The ways of fate are mysterious, and all actions are rewarded.*

"The truth of these three precepts was evidenced in the story of the ankle bracelet, hence our poem shall be titled *The Lay of the Ankle Bracelet.*

"The moral lesson to be drawn from this story is important for the three kings who rule the three kingdoms. It appears, venerable saint, that you would be the one most qualified to write this great story."

In answer to Shâttan's request, the saint, whose renown has remained unequaled, composed a poem in thirty cantos, the subjects of which are the following:

The Blessings. The Installation of a Home. A Description of Mâdhavi, Receiving from the King the Honors She Deserved for her Great Success on the Stage. The Evening's Splendor. Indra's Festival. The Joys of the Seashore. Songs on the Seashore. Mâdhavi's Sorrow. The Desert's Heat. A Description of the City and of the Forest. The Hunter's Song. Kôvalan and his Wife Stay in the Suburbs. The Sights of Madurai. The Refuge Found for Charming Kannaki. Kôvalan's Murder. The Dance of the Cowgirls. The Despair of People when the City was Burnt. The Town during the Conflagration. The

Pleading of Kannaki before the King. The Revenge. Description of the Disaster. Secrets Revealed to Kannaki by the Goddess of Madurai. The Dance of the Mountain Girls. The Stone Bathed in the Sacred Ganges. The Consecration of the Image. The Offerings to the Goddess of Faithfulness and the Blessings Obtained from her.

The great events told by Shâttan, who belonged to the caste of grain merchants of Madurai, have been woven into a long poem, interspersed with songs, by Prince Ilangô Adigal, to illustrate the three precepts stated in this preamble.

APPENDIX II

Uraiperukatturai

After these events, the Pândya kingdom no longer received the blessings of rain and was devastated by a famine, soon followed by fever and plague.

King Verrivêrcheliyan,* who ruled from Korkai, was able to appease the new goddess of Faithfulness by sacrificing thousands of goldsmiths and celebrating a festival in her honor. Rain came back, and, with it, peace and prosperity on earth. The kingdom was freed from misery and pestilence.

When he heard this story, Ilam-Kôshar, king of Kongu-nâdu, arranged a similar festival, and rains in abundance came to his country.

Then King Gajabâhu, in his sea-girt island of Ceylon, built a temple consecrated to the goddess of Faithfulness. In the hope that she might drive away all evils, he offered rich sacrifices before her altar every day; he also created a festival during the first month of the year. The rains came in time, and the fertile earth produced an abundant harvest.

The Chôla named Perumkilli built in Uraiyûr a sanctuary to this goddess of Chastity. Each day new offerings were brought to her altar in the hope that she would grant her blessings and gifts to the country for all ages to come.

* Successor to the Pândya king of the poem

New Directions Paperbooks

Walter Abish, *Alphabetical Africa*. NDP375.
Ilangô Adigal, *Shilappadikaram*. NDP162.
Brother Antoninus, *The Residual Years*. NDP263.
Guillaume Apollinaire, *Selected Writings*.† NDP310.
Djuna Barnes, *Nightwood*. NDP98.
Charles Baudelaire, *Flowers of Evil*.† NDP71.
Paris Spleen. NDP294.
Gottfried Benn, *Primal Vision*. NDP322.
Eric Bentley, *Bernard Shaw*. NDP59.
Wolfgang Borchert, *The Man Outside*. NDP319.
Jorge Luis Borges, *Labyrinths*. NDP186.
Jean-François Bory, *Once Again*. NDP256.
Kay Boyle, *Thirty Stories*. NDP62.
E. Brock, *Invisibility Is The Art of Survival*. NDP342.
The Portraits & The Poses. NDP360.
W. Bronk, *The World, the Worldless*. NDP157.
Buddha, *The Dhammapada*. NDP188.
Hayden Carruth, *For You*. NDP298.
From Snow and Rock, from Chaos. NDP349.
Louis-Ferdinand Céline,
Death on the Installment Plan. NDP330.
Guignol's Band. NDP278.
Journey to the End of the Night. NDP84.
Blaise Cendrars, *Selected Writings*.† NDP203.
B-c. Chatterjee, *Krishnakanta's Will*. NDP120.
Jean Cocteau, *The Holy Terrors*. NDP212.
The Infernal Machine. NDP235.
M. Cohen, *Monday Rhetoric*. NDP352.
Cid Corman, *Livingdying*. NDP289.
Sun Rock Man. NDP318.
Gregory Corso, *Elegiac Feelings American*. NDP299.
Long Live Man. NDP127.
Happy Birthday of Death. NDP86.
Edward Dahlberg, *Reader*. NDP246.
Because I Was Flesh. NDP227.
David Daiches, *Virginia Woolf*.
(Revised) NDP96.
Osamu Dazai, *The Setting Sun*. NDP258.
No Longer Human. NDP357.
Coleman Dowell, *Mrs. October Was Here*. NDP368.
Robert Duncan, *Roots and Branches*. NDP275.
Bending the Bow. NDP255.
The Opening of the Field. NDP356.
Richard Eberhart, *Selected Poems*. NDP198.
Russell Edson, *The Very Thing That Happens*. NDP137.
Wm. Empson, *7 Types of Ambiguity*. NDP204.
Some Versions of Pastoral. NDP92.
Wm. Everson, *The Residual Years*. NDP263.
Man-Fate. NDP369.
Lawrence Ferlinghetti, *Her*. NDP88.
Back Roads to Far Places. NDP312.
A Coney Island of the Mind. NDP74.
The Mexican Night. NDP300.
Open Eye, Open Heart. NDP361.
Routines. NDP187.
The Secret Meaning of Things. NDP268.
Starting from San Francisco. NDP 220.
Tyrannus Nix?. NDP288.
Ronald Firbank, *Two Novels*. NDP128.
Dudley Fitts,
Poems from the Greek Anthology. NDP60.
F. Scott Fitzgerald, *The Crack-up*. NDP54.
Robert Fitzgerald, *Spring Shade: Poems 1931-1970*. NDP311.
Gustave Flaubert,
Bouvard and Pécuchet. NDP328.
The Dictionary of Accepted Ideas. NDP230.
M. K. Gandhi, *Gandhi on Non-Violence*.
(ed. Thomas Merton) NDP197.
André Gide, *Dostoevsky*. NDP100.
Goethe, *Faust*, Part I.
(MacIntyre translation) NDP70.

Albert J. Guerard, *Thomas Hardy*. NDP185.
Guillevic, *Selected Poems*. NDP279.
Henry Hatfield, *Goethe*. NDP136.
Thomas Mann. (Revised Edition) NDP101.
John Hawkes, *The Cannibal*. NDP123.
The Lime Twig. NDP95.
Second Skin. NDP146.
The Beetle Leg. NDP239.
The Blood Oranges. NDP338.
The Innocent Party. NDP238.
Lunar Landscapes. NDP274.
A. Hayes, *A Wreath of Christmas Poems*. NDP347.
H.D., *Hermetic Definition*. NDP343.
Trilogy. NDP362.
Hermann Hesse, *Siddhartha*. NDP65.
Christopher Isherwood, *The Berlin Stories*. NDP134.
Gustav Janouch,
Conversations With Kafka. NDP313.
Alfred Jarry, *Ubu Roi*. NDP105.
Robinson Jeffers, *Cawdor and Medea*. NDP293.
James Joyce, *Stephen Hero*. NDP133.
James Joyce/Finnegans Wake. NDP331.
Franz Kafka, *Amerika*. NDP117.
Bob Kaufman,
Solitudes Crowded with Loneliness. NDP199.
Hugh Kenner, *Wyndham Lewis*. NDP167.
Kenyon Critics, *Gerard Manley Hopkins*. NDP355.
P. Lal, translator, *Great Sanskrit Plays*. NDP142.
Tommaso Landolfi,
Gogol's Wife and Other Stories. NDP155.
Lautréamont, *Maldoror*. NDP207.
Denise Levertov, *Footprints*. NDP344.
The Jacob's Ladder. NDP112.
The Poet in the World. NDP363.
O Taste and See. NDP149.
Relearning the Alphabet. NDP290.
The Sorrow Dance. NDP222.
To Stay Alive. NDP325.
With Eyes at the Back of Our Heads. NDP229.
Harry Levin, *James Joyce*. NDP87.
García Lorca, *Selected Poems*.† NDP114.
Three Tragedies. NDP52.
Five Plays. NDP232.
Michael McClure, *September Blackberries*. NDP370.
Carson McCullers, *The Member of the Wedding*. (Playscript) NDP153.
Thomas Merton, *Cables to the Ace*. NDP252.
Emblems of a Season of Fury. NDP140.
Gandhi on Non-Violence. NDP197.
The Geography of Lograire. NDP283.
New Seeds of Contemplation. NDP337.
Raids on the Unspeakable. NDP213.
Selected Poems. NDP85.
The Way of Chuang Tzu. NDP276.
The Wisdom of the Desert. NDP295.
Zen and the Birds of Appetite. NDP261.
Henri Michaux, *Selected Writings*.† NDP264.
Henry Miller, *The Air-Conditioned Nightmare*. NDP302.
Big Sur & The Oranges of Hieronymus Bosch. NDP161.
The Books in My Life. NDP280.
The Colossus of Maroussi. NDP75.
The Cosmological Eye. NDP109.
Henry Miller on Writing. NDP151.
The Henry Miller Reader. NDP269.
Remember to Remember. NDP111.
Stand Still Like the Hummingbird. NDP236.
The Time of the Assassins. NDP115.
The Wisdom of the Heart. NDP94.
Y. Mishima, *Death in Midsummer*. NDP215.
Confessions of a Mask. NDP253.
Eugenio Montale, *Selected Poems*.† NDP193.

Vladimir Nabokov, *Nikolai Gogol.* NDP78.
P. Neruda, *The Captain's Verses.*† NDP345.
   Residence on Earth.† NDP340.
New Directions 17. (Anthology) NDP103.
New Directions 18. (Anthology) NDP163.
New Directions 19. (Anthology) NDP214.
New Directions 20. (Anthology) NDP248.
New Directions 21. (Anthology) NDP277.
New Directions 22. (Anthology) NDP291.
New Directions 23. (Anthology) NDP315.
New Directions 24. (Anthology) NDP332.
New Directions 25. (Anthology) NDP339.
New Directions 26. (Anthology) NDP353.
New Directions 27. (Anthology) NDP359.
New Directions 28. (Anthology) NDP371.
Charles Olson, *Selected Writings.* NDP231.
George Oppen, *The Materials.* NDP122.
   Of Being Numerous. NDP245.
   This In Which. NDP201.
Wilfred Owen, *Collected Poems.* NDP210.
Nicanor Parra, *Emergency Poems.*† NDP333.
   Poems and Antipoems.† NDP242.
Boris Pasternak, *Safe Conduct.* NDP77.
Kenneth Patchen, *Aflame and Afun of*
   Walking Faces. NDP292.
   Because It Is. NDP83.
   But Even So. NDP265.
   Collected Poems. NDP284.
   Doubleheader. NDP211.
   Hallelujah Anyway. NDP219.
   In Quest of Candlelighters. NDP334.
   The Journal of Albion Moonlight. NDP99.
   Memoirs of a Shy Pornographer. NDP205.
   Selected Poems. NDP160.
   Sleepers Awake. NDP286.
   Wonderings. NDP320.
Octavio Paz, *Configurations.*† NDP303.
   Early Poems.† NDP354.
Plays for a New Theater. (Anth.) NDP216.
Ezra Pound, *ABC of Reading.* NDP89.
   Classic Noh Theatre of Japan. NDP79.
   The Confucian Odes. NDP81.
   Confucius. NDP285.
   Confucius to Cummings. (Anth.) NDP126.
   Guide to Kulchur. NDP257.
   Literary Essays. NDP250.
   Love Poems of Ancient Egypt. Gift Edition.
   NDP178.
   Pound/Joyce. NDP296.
   Selected Cantos. NDP304.
   Selected Letters 1907-1941. NDP317.
   Selected Poems. NDP66.
   The Spirit of Romance. NDP266.
   Translations.† (Enlarged Edition) NDP145.
Omar Pound, *Arabic and Persian Poems.*
   NDP305.
James Purdy, *Children Is All.* NDP327.
Raymond Queneau, *The Bark Tree.* NDP314.
   The Flight of Icarus. NDP358.
Carl Rakosi, *Amulet.* NDP234.
   Ere-Voice. NDP321.
M. Randall, *Part of the Solution.* NDP350.
John Crowe Ransom, *Beating the Bushes.*
   NDP324.
Raja Rao, *Kanthapura.* NDP224.
Herbert Read, *The Green Child.* NDP208.
P. Reverdy, *Selected Poems.*† NDP346.
Kenneth Rexroth, *Assays.* NDP113.
   An Autobiographical Novel. NDP281.
   Bird in the Bush. NDP80.
   Collected Longer Poems. NDP309.
   Collected Shorter Poems. NDP243.
   Love and the Turning Year. NDP308.
   100 Poems from the Chinese. NDP192.
   100 Poems from the Japanese.† NDP147.

Charles Reznikoff, *By the Waters of Manhattan.*
   NDP121.
   Testimony: The United States 1885-1890.
   NDP200.
Arthur Rimbaud, *Illuminations.*† NDP56.
   Season in Hell & Drunken Boat.† NDP97.
Selden Rodman, *Tongues of Fallen Angels.*
   NDP373.
Saikaku Ihara, *The Life of an Amorous*
   Woman. NDP270.
St. John of the Cross, *Poems.*† NDP341.
Jean-Paul Sartre, *Baudelaire.* NDP233.
   Nausea. NDP82.
   The Wall (Intimacy). NDP272.
Delmore Schwartz, *Selected Poems.* NDP241.
Stevie Smith, *Selected Poems.* NDP159.
Gary Snyder, *The Back Country.* NDP249.
   Earth House Hold. NDP267.
   Regarding Wave. NDP306.
Gilbert Sorrentino, *Splendide-Hotel.* NDP364.
Enid Starkie, *Arthur Rimbaud.* NDP254.
Stendhal, *Lucien Leuwen.*
   Book II: *The Telegraph.* NDP108.
Jules Supervielle, *Selected Writings.*† NDP209.
W. Sutton, *American Free Verse.* NDP351.
Dylan Thomas, *Adventures in the Skin Trade.*
   NDP183.
   A Child's Christmas in Wales. Gift Edition.
   NDP181.
   Collected Poems 1934-1952. NDP316.
   The Doctor and the Devils. NDP297.
   Portrait of the Artist as a Young Dog.
   NDP51.
   Quite Early One Morning. NDP90.
   Under Milk Wood. NDP73.
Lionel Trilling, *E. M. Forster.* NDP189.
Martin Turnell, *Art of French Fiction.* NDP251.
   Baudelaire. NDP336.
Paul Valéry, *Selected Writings.*† NDP184.
Elio Vittorini, *Twilight of the Elephant.* NDP366.
   Women of Messina. NDP365.
Vernon Watkins, *Selected Poems.* NDP221.
Nathanael West, *Miss Lonelyhearts &*
   Day of the Locust. NDP125.
George F. Whicher, tr.,
   The Goliard Poets.† NDP206.
J. Willett, *Theatre of Bertolt Brecht.* NDP244.
J. Williams, *An Ear in Bartram's Tree.* NDP335.
Tennessee Williams, *Hard Candy.* NDP225.
   Camino Real. NDP301.
   Dragon Country. NDP287.
   Eight Mortal Ladies Possessed. NDP374.
   The Glass Menagerie. NDP218.
   In the Winter of Cities. NDP154.
   One Arm & Other Stories. NDP237.
   Out Cry. NDP367.
   The Roman Spring of Mrs. Stone. NDP271.
   Small Craft Warnings. NDP348.
   27 Wagons Full of Cotton. NDP217.
William Carlos Williams,
   The William Carlos Williams Reader.
   NDP282.
   The Autobiography. NDP223.
   The Build-up. NDP259.
   The Farmers' Daughters. NDP106.
   Imaginations. NDP329.
   In the American Grain. NDP53.
   In the Money. NDP240.
   Many Loves. NDP191.
   Paterson. Complete. NDP152.
   Pictures from Brueghel. NDP118.
   The Selected Essays. NDP273.
   Selected Poems. NDP131.
   A Voyage to Pagany. NDP307.
   White Mule. NDP226.
Yvor Winters,
   Edwin Arlington Robinson. NDP326.

Complete descriptive catalog available free on request from
New Directions, 333 Sixth Avenue, New York 10014.   † Bilingual.